PRIZE SURPRISE SWEEPSTAKES!

This month's prize:

A FABULOUS SHARP VIEWCAM!

This month, as a special surprise, we're giving away a Sharp ViewCam**, the big-screen camcorder that has revolutionized home videos!

This is the camcorder everyone's talking about! Sharp's new ViewCam has a big 3" full-color viewing screen with 180° swivel action that lets you control everything you record—and watch it at the same time! Features include a remote control (so you can get into the picture yourself), 8 power zoom, full-range auto focus, battery pack, recharger and more!

The next page contains two Entry Coupons (as does every book you received this shipment). Complete and return *all* the entry coupons; **the more times you enter, the better your chances of winning!**

Then keep your fingers crossed, because you'll find out by November 15, 1995 if you're the winner!

Remember: The more times you enter, the better your chances of winning!*

*NO PURCHASE OR OBLIGATION TO CONTINUE BEING A SUBSCRIBER NECESSARY TO ENTER. SEE THE BACK PAGE FOR ALTERNATE MEANS OF ENTRY, AND RULES.

**THE PROPRIETORS OF THE TRADEMARK ARE NOT ASSOCIATED WITH THIS PROMOTION.

PRIZE SURPRISE
SWEEPSTAKES

OFFICIAL ENTRY COUPON

This entry must be received by: OCTOBER 30, 1995
This month's winner will be notified by: NOVEMBER 15, 1995

YES, I want to win the Sharp ViewCam! Please enter me in the drawing and let me know if I've won!

Name_____

Address _____ Apt. _____

City   State/Prov.   Zip/Postal Code

Account #_____

Return entry with invoice in reply envelope.

© 1995 HARLEQUIN ENTERPRISES LTD.   CVC KAL

PRIZE SURPRISE
SWEEPSTAKES

OFFICIAL ENTRY COUPON

This entry must be received by: OCTOBER 30, 1995
This month's winner will be notified by: NOVEMBER 15, 1995

YES, I want to win the Sharp ViewCam! Please enter me in the drawing and let me know if I've won!

Name_____

Address _____ Apt. _____

City   State/Prov.   Zip/Postal Code

Account #_____

Return entry with invoice in reply envelope.

© 1995 HARLEQUIN ENTERPRISES LTD.   CVC KAL

"Sex is not a reason for marriage!" Amy spluttered.

"It's a good foundation," West replied. "But we've so much more. You attract me, and vice versa. As a breeding pair we are a match!"

"You make us sound like a pair of rabbits!" she protested.

"Not discriminating enough!" He laughed, and his fingers lifted her hair. "You know I've been wanting to touch you, to kiss you, to make love to you."

Rosalie Henaghan grew up on the family farm in New Zealand. As a child, she saw nothing exotic in feeding cattle, mustering sheep, checking stock or tramping in the bush. Trained as a teacher, Rosalie entered radio, where she had her own daily program. Writing and editing scripts developed her storytelling ability and, interviewing author Essie Summers, Rosalie received encouragement to "sit down and write...."

Love, Desire and You
Rosalie Henaghan

Harlequin Books

TORONTO • NEW YORK • LONDON
AMSTERDAM • PARIS • SYDNEY • HAMBURG
STOCKHOLM • ATHENS • TOKYO • MILAN
MADRID • WARSAW • BUDAPEST • AUCKLAND

ISBN 0-373-17253-2

LOVE, DESIRE AND YOU

First North American Publication 1995.

This edition published by arrangement with Harlequin Books S.A.

® and TM are trademarks of the publisher. Trademarks indicated with
® are registered in the United States Patent and Trademark Office, the
Canadian Trade Marks Office and in other countries.

Printed in U.S.A.

CHAPTER ONE

'STOP that! What do you think you're doing?'

Amy Radcliffe, fingers deep in the soil as she lifted a clump of daffodil bulbs, paused in surprise. In the evening peace of the valley, the accusing voice grated. Looking up, she saw a dark-haired man vault the adjoining fence and advance with the purpose of a prosecutor. Conscious of her isolation, Amy frowned as she wiped a wisp of brown hair from her face with the back of her hand, and her hazel eyes shadowed as she noted the size of the intruder. The man was big and moved with aggressive power. Lowering the bulbs, Amy grabbed the garden fork and calculated the distance between her car and the man.

'Plant thieves are slugs!' he shouted. 'Gastropods!'

'I've two feet, do not move in slime and my stomach is a long way from the ground!' Amy was ready to run but the man stopped by her car and, to her chagrin, she saw amusement on his face as he mentally measured her statement and her five feet ten inches. Irritated, but satisfied she was not in danger, Amy lowered the fork, the vicious prongs glinting silver sharp, an unsubtle hint that the length of her legs was not his affair. Had she imagined the smile admitting an apology?

She strove for dignity, regretting her grubby appearance, her old blouse, baggy shorts and gardening boots while her opponent, in brown leather jacket, open-necked shirt, cream moleskin trousers and polished tan shoes wasn't even breathing fast after his run. His glance went beyond her to the precise patchwork marked by the line-up of bulbs in their numbered containers, and the design it revealed. She saw his expression harden, his eyes flash, burning her with contempt.

'You're not an opportunist after a few plants!' he savaged. 'Somehow you found out the pattern Miss Radcliffe used. The last results of more than fifty years of plant hybridisation! You've waited for the optimum moment to lift the bulbs and you've cross-numbered each one. Obviously, you know exactly what you are doing. You disgust me!' He reached through an open window of her old hatchback to remove her keys. 'You won't get far without transport out here.'

The whiplash of his authority had reduced Amy to slack-jawed silence, but the pocketing of her keys stung. 'Those are my keys! Give them back!'

'When I'm ready. First, you can carry those bulbs in their containers into my first packing shed, on the other side of the hedge. Now, get moving!'

The reference to his packing shed told her his identity. She realised she should have guessed from his proprietorial stance. 'Dr Westleigh Thornton, I presume?' Her voice was saccharin over acid. 'May I ask what you intend doing with the bulbs, once they are in your possession?'

'You have asked, but I don't intend to answer. It's none of your business!'

'It is my business!' she stormed up to him. 'My name is Amy Jean Radcliffe and I was bequeathed this property by my great-aunt. I was looking forward to meeting you—my aunt mentioned you frequently. Now I'm wondering if you had a more devious intent. I find you——' she paused for an insult and remembered one of her aunt's '—an ill-mannered academic with atrophied common sense.'

His look of astonishment give way to a rich chuckle.

'You're Jean Radcliffe's great-niece, all right!' He reached forward to shake her hand, disarming her by thrusting the fork into the next row. 'I should have guessed. Not many answer me back. I never thought I'd meet another individual with the style of Aunt Jean. Such a wonderful, independent woman. My brother Jonathan and I loved her dearly.' His smile, reflective and gentle, revealed the beauty of his dark eyes. Amy could not doubt his sincerity.

'We'd better start again, Amy Jean Radcliffe. Go through the charade of mutual apology. Aunt Jean was an excellent neighbour with our family all her life. I was four when someone said she wasn't my "proper" aunt and I was quite vehement that she was. Fortunately, she explained that some women had the gift of being aunties through love, and that satisfied me.' His glance went to the daffodil bulbs. 'Aunt Jean's experiments in plant hybridisation fascinated me. It was through her that I became interested in plant research.'

'She was very proud of you.' Amy admitted. 'When you were granted your doctorate in plant genetics, I read every detail in her letters. Your success in floriculture thrilled her, Dr Thornton.'

'Call me West. Aunt Jean was my first consultant. She advised which varieties of gladioli and chrysanthemums would do well in our soil. When we had ongoing marketing problems, she encouraged me to open my first nursery and florist's shop.' He looked towards the deepening purple of the hills. 'I would have been at her funeral, but I didn't hear the news until I returned to Port Moresby.'

'Your letter explained. Searching for new orchid

varieties in the highlands of Papua New Guinea. Aunt Jean told me she said goodbye, after you'd been at our home to visit her on your way north. I was sorry I was at work and didn't meet you.'

'You'd met Jonathon, years ago. I remember being quite miffed that Aunt Jean's wonderful Amy had been to stay again and I'd been away.'

'School holidays are at the same time! As a child, I loved coming to the South Island and the cottage in the country every summer. I never intended to stay away so long. It's been six years. While I was at varsity, I worked during the holidays to make some money. Aunt Jean would come to Auckland and stay with us. When I went overseas, she joined me a couple of times.'

'The Chelsea Flower Show! We were meant to meet there.'

'Aunt Jean and I laughed about it, when you didn't turn up.'

'My fault. I delayed my flight out of Singapore as I had to instruct a new staff member about our export orders. By the time I arrived in England I was tired from sitting on an airliner for so long.'

'Someone said you were as scratchy as blackberry canes after long flights!'

'Sounds like Sue, my brother Jonathon's wife. You've met her?'

'At the funeral a month ago, and again at lunchtime today. I rang and told them I was coming, so Sue opened up the cottage, switched on the hot water and so on. She told me you had arranged someone to keep the irrigation checked and the lawns in order. I must pay you.'

'Forget it. How long are you here?'

'I've taken three weeks from work. Aunt Jean's

affairs can't be finalised until the bulb orders are sent.
I promised her that I'd take care of everything.'

'Ask me for any help you need. I'm not usually such
a boor—as Sue said, long flights don't suit me. I just
flew in from Los Angeles and thought I'd check my
office lab before I went home to bed. A few hours'
sleep and my body clock slips back into place, but
when I saw you. . .'

'Raiding Aunt Jean's precious bulbs! You frightened
me.'

'You looked like Boadicea, trident and all!' he
chuckled. 'I'd better report in; my staff are probably
wondering where I disappeared. I'll call in on you
tomorrow.'

Amy acknowledged his departure with a smile. Dr
Westleigh Thornton with his intelligent dark eyes and
wavy black hair was even more good-looking than his
equally tall, sandy-haired brother. Both had filled out
from the photo on Aunt Jean's dressing-table of two
teenage schoolboys with large knees, praying mantis
legs and spider arms! It was not a surprise when her
great-aunt's solicitor had told her that Jonathon and
Westleigh Thornton were to receive small gifts from
the estate. Jonathon had been left a fine old sideboard
from the parlour, but West was to select half the
record, tape and compact disc collection. Equally, it
was not a surprise to be told that West Thornton had
offered a more than fair price for the old stone cottage
and the plants and the ten hectares she had been left.
Amy had told the solicitor she would probably accept
West's offer.

Since arriving at the cottage after lunch she had
become less sure, less certain she wanted to part with
the old stone house. It was sound economic sense to
sell it—living just out of Auckland, she was close to

her family and work—but she had forgotten how lovely the cottage was, situated on the sunny side of the low valley, its clover honey-coloured stone mellow against the backdrop of gardens and orchards. Standing at the front door, she could look down the valley and in the distance was the sea. The cottage had been built by her great-grandfather, a stonemason and farmer from England, after he had prospered in New Zealand. Her grandparents had lived in the cottage and her father had been born in the front bedroom, a precious link as she hardly remembered him, a shadowy, tall figure who had died when she was four. Great-aunt Jean had stayed on in the cottage, her only paternal relative.

Her mother had remarried and Amy had willingly accepted the love of her stepfather and later, the arrival of another sister and brother. Great-aunt Jean had always been her 'special' aunt; each had treasured the holidays at the cottage and the frequent visits when her great-aunt came to stay, but the distance and the barrier of Cook Strait, as well as her aunt's busy life, had imposed limits.

On arrival Amy had opened up the cottage and wandered round; the tidy rooms needed redecorating, but they were full of sunshine and she could almost hear her great-aunt's laughter and brisk steps. Amy studied the large portraits on the walls in the 'front room', the carefully hand-painted photographs of earlier generations. She could see her resemblance to her father and he, in turn, was like his father and Aunt Jean. Gaze honest and direct, the full-lower-lipped smile hinting at passion and humour, their figures tall and sturdy, their feet firm on the ground. Looking at the portrait of her green-eyed grandmother, Amy coveted her delicate beauty. No doubt Dr Westleigh

Thornton could tell why she, Amy, was a daughter of the soil, instead of a creature of the air!

Outside, her aunt's garden was still beautiful. The lawns were mown and the trickle irrigation on, but no attempt had been made to trim back the summer's profligate growth or remove weeds. *Alyssum maritimum*, forget-me-nots and pansies had infiltrated the meandering paths. The garden had once featured herbaceous borders and there remained a collection of perennials. Aunt's passion for daffodils showed in the two paddocks in the front of the house. The trees and shrubs had been left to grow. A magnificent copper beech tree set well back from the property glowed in the sunlight and led her scrutiny to the woodland— hundred-year-old oaks, limes and elms her great grandparents had nurtured from seed. In front of her was the red photinia hedge and, following it to the rear, Amy found the tangle of pumpkins, parsley, basil and strawberries which had been the kitchen garden. Munching on some of the ripe purple-black grapes, she picked and pocketed some passionfruit as she pushed her way through the vines, searching for the enclosed rose garden she had designed as a student project. Aunt Jean's construction of the garden had been an encouragement and the garden had just been planted before the road accident which had smashed her aunt's left knee four years earlier. The decision to close the gate had been forced by pain, Aunt Jean's efforts concentrated on the daffodils.

A wall of shrubs and trees, rivalling that around Sleeping Beauty's castle, protected the outer circle and Amy found the gate, because she had stopped to enjoy the picture of red and gold nasturtiums coiled and matted around a pigeonwood which had grown through the slatted gate.

Smiling at her own secret garden, she had to return to the garden shed to find a saw and secateurs. Despite the protesting pungency of the nasturtiums, Amy soon had access, and her reward. She had designed the garden in an open rose shape, ever-widening petal beds separated by camomile lawn. Red roses of every variety bloomed in a tangle of growth, but the camomile kept some form. Amy picked her way, snipping back protruding branches, identifying favourites and revelling in the scents of crushed camomile and roses, the perfume of late summer. On reaching the centre rows, it was a visual relief to see white roses.

Walking through to the far side, Amy realised the end roses were a hotchpotch, many of which she could not name. Most were poor specimens, some more pink than red, but one hybrid tea bush stood out, a mass of red blooms, each one a champion. She looked at the bush in admiration. The colour was a singing rich red, the necks holding the heads proudly, the stems straight, long and almost thornless. From where she stood, she breathed in the fragrance.

'The symbol of love! The perfect red rose! Magnificent! I don't recognise you, but I know more about old roses than the modern varieties.' Her thoughts were spoken aloud and Amy glanced back, feeling silly, glad no one had heard. She secateured one perfect, long-stemmed bud. Returning to the cottage, she steeped it in a tall glass, added some open lemonade from her journey and took it upstairs to her bedroom. Until she located the vases, the glass would suffice, but such a bud deserved crystal.

Upstairs she made up her bed in her old bedroom, and then the promise to her aunt encouraged her outside to start on the task of lifting the bulbs. There had been no trouble locating them from the field plan her aunt had drawn, and the almost buried numbers had matched the empty, prepared cartons in the garden shed. She had worked steadily and meticulously for two hours, until West Thornton's interruption.

Stretching arms above her head, easing her muscles, she decided to stop work. Daylight was fading, she was tired from her long drive the previous day and the morning's journey, but more fatigued by the swirling emotions her aunt's cottage had activated. She wished her young sister or brother had accompanied her, but with exams due, it had not been sensible to disturb their studies. Carting the boxes of bulbs into the hatchback, intending to use it as a barrow to cart them to the shed, took only minutes. With her training it was impossible not to clean the implements and she set them also in the rear of the car and, with a satisfied sigh, slipped into the driver's seat and reached for the keys.

The keys! West Thornton had pocketed them and they had both forgotten his action. Hidden behind the macrocarpa hedge were the packing sheds and glasshouses of the West Thornton empire, and beyond that his flower fields. Further down the valley was the large homestead where Jonathon, Sue and their three children lived and where West had his own wing.

Would West be checking his domain? At least she could lock the car doors without keys. Completing it, she headed for the gate in the fence and the gap in the boundary hedge. Once through, she was staggered by the size, the rows of glass-houses a crystal village, the shade houses impressive, and higher up was a postmodern structure, the administration centre. As she stood staring, she saw the sign, 'Guard dogs on duty'. Urgent, querulous baying made Amy decide that searching for West would be an adventure she could forgo. Running, she fled through the gap, seized and shut the gate, backache forgotten. Memories of guard dogs at nurseries on the Continent were vivid.

Safe in her own field, she stopped by her car. The vehicle would be in view from her kitchen and soon night would hide it. As the cottage and the West Thornton property were at the end of the road, there was little risk of passers-by, so she decided to walk down to the homestead to retrieve the keys after she had bathed and put on some more presentable clothes.

Amy washed away the worst of the dirt at the outside tub, the water cold on her skin. The bathroom of the cottage was off the kitchen-living area, an arrangement dating back to the time when the wood range had heated the water. Although the water system had been modernised by her great-aunt, the bathroom kept some of its original glory. In the centre of the floor on a raised dais of slate was a huge, deep, claw-footed bath. Angled over one end were two pipes for hot and cold but their taps were gleaming brass dragons. To set the water frothing from their capacious mouths, Amy pushed down their tails, smiling with joy. How could she have forgotten the marvellous taps? After the rust-splattered orange coughed, faded and cleared, she inserted the plug and added a lavish amount of bubble bath, before turning aside to the basin to scrub the caked dirt from her fingernails, making a mental note to buy gardening gloves on her first visit to the nearest store. She freed her long brown hair, brushed it and then went back to the living area to switch on the compact disc player. Scanning the discs took time—one of her aunt's passions had been music, opera in particular, and a lifetime's collection of records, tapes and, in latter years, compact discs occupied a floor-to-ceiling cupboard. Selecting *The Mastersingers of Nuremberg*, Amy thought appropriate—her aunt had treated her to the opera while they were in Germany. The volume was satisfyingly sensuous, easily overpowering the noise of the hot water.

The bath ready, she threw off the remainder of her clothes and lowered her stiffening body into the layers of bubbles and foam. With a sigh of sybaritic indulgence, she let the warm water seep over her, stranding and darkening her shoulder-length hair. It was, she decided one of life's great pleasures. . .to lie in a bath unhurried, toes on taps allowing the water to remain hot, knowing she had all the time she wanted. . . drowning in glorious sound.

The volume lessening was the first intimation that she was no longer alone. West Thornton was leaning lazily against the open bathroom door, his dark eyes agleam with laughter. Startled, she sat up, then slid back up to her neck into the water, causing a wave which sent water cascading over the rim on to the floor.

'One of life's pleasures, a hot bath after hard work,' he echoed her earlier thought, 'but watching a beautiful woman take a bath is even better. Of course, sharing it would be best!'

'What are you doing here? Please leave!'

'I came to bring back your keys.' He dangled them. 'You could have bolted the door. I did knock and I called out before I walked in, but *The Mastersingers* told me you were in. Don't panic—thanks to the foam, I have to admit more can be seen every summer's day on Tahunanui beach! Now, to business. I've driven your car into the garage and locked it. The bulbs should be safe enough there for one night.'

Amy nodded agreement and tried to sink down lower.

'Degas must have been a misogynist when he painted his *Woman in a Bath* series. Miss Radcliffe, you are breathtakingly lovely in that setting.'

Amy scrabbled for the flannel and her dignity. The foam was beginning to dissipate. 'Please, I am not in the habit of entertaining in my bath.'

'I assure you it's a respectable thing to do, quite royal, in fact. Remember the Order of the Bath!' His grin was wolfish. 'Jonathon and Sue have probably told you that if you have difficulty sleeping, you're welcome down at the house. I'd like to endorse that sentiment, and offer an alternative, I could stay here with you.' His smile was elaborate innocence. 'No? I'd like to make up for our introduction. Should I add some more hot water? Rub your back?'

'Come one step closer and I'll slosh you,' Amy warned.

'With the foam or the flannel!' he chuckled. 'I shouldn't take advantage of a woman in vulnerable circumstances, but you look so gloriously sensual, those smooth, creamy-pink shoulders hinting erotically of deeper delights. . .and those cute toes. . . I'll stop teasing. I know the phone was switched off here, so I've put my mobile phone on the table. It's fully charged. In the morning, leave it in the letterbox and I'll recharge it again and return it later. Push memory and one for my lab and flat, memory and two will call Jonathon and Sue. We'll talk tomorrow.'

He smiled, a flash of white teeth, dark eyes alight, and then moved away. Amy glared after him.

'Enjoy your bath, Aphrodite!'

She heard the click of the outer door and knew she

was alone. There was, she decided, a lot to be said for showers.

Amy yawned as she listened to her small radio. The ten o'clock news had just started but she was so tired she barely comprehended its content. Snuggled into the comfortable bed, she reached up to switch off her bedside light. A faint, snuffling noise disturbed her, but she guessed it was a hedgehog rooting among the plants below her bedroom window. She was just about asleep when a crying wail sounded from the direction of the back door. Never had she heard such a pitiful, ghostly howl!

Alert and alarmed, she flicked on the light, and the sound stopped. Her mind screened through too many lurid scenarios, but she comforted herself by the feel of the smoothness of the phone. Simply knowing help was available if necessary calmed her as she grabbed her dressing-gown. Listening hard, she heard a faint whimpering, like someone in distress.

It was an additional reassurance to look out the stairs window and see the lights of the Thornton house further down the valley. Keeping back from the kitchen door, she called out. The whimpering stopped but a panting and scratching noise almost had her hair standing on end. Switching on the outside light she lifted the curtain of the side window. A lumpy dog pleaded, its tail beginning a triumphant drum-roll. She slipped the door-chain to its length, wide enough for the skinny dog to enter. 'You gave me the worst fright of my life! Worse than the gothic movie I saw when I was thirteen!' Amy scolded. 'Where did you come from? And don't look at me like that—as soon as I find out where you belong, you're going straight back!' She viewed her foundling with some dismay. 'Poor thing! You're half starved, by the look of you. My guess is you're a stray someone's dumped at the end of the road. I'll give you a drink and find some food, then I'll make you up a box in the laundry.'

As she spoke, she shut the door and rebolted the chain. She found an empty plastic ice-cream container and filled it with water, but after a couple of cursory licks, two large, golden eyes stared up at her. She fondled the grey, wiry hair. 'You might be a bag of bones, but you have beautiful eyes,' she chuckled as the creature ambled towards the refrigerator.

'All right, I can see you're hungry, but I don't feel like giving you this fine steak my neighbour's left me. You think your need is greater than mine, I suppose!' She cut some meat off the side, conscious of golden eyes leering appreciatively and the tail again thumping with expectation. The meat disappeared with speed and the golden eyes begged for more. She cut up half but put the rest away, knowing that the dog would require food in the morning. After nosing the plate around the room to gain every morsel, the dog watched as she found rags and made a shape with an old sheepskin. He inspected and sniffed it, circled three times then settled, yawning with contentment. Relieved and intrigued, Amy switched off the lights and went back to bed.

In the morning, she woke to a rough tongue licking her feet. Startled, she jerked and a yelp refreshed her memory. Two golden, trusting eyes blinked at her.

'What are you doing in my bed? If you've got fleas, I'll be. . .' The thought was enough to propel her out of bed. The dog raced ahead of her, down the stairs to the back door and she opened it, mindful of puddles and worse, realising she knew nothing about house-training animals. He returned, paws damp with the dew, skating on the old linoleum. Amy laughed at his indignant expression, but she shifted a couple of the mats to give him purchase and he licked her hand.

'You look dog-sized but I think you're just a puppy! An ungainly, lumpy puppy at that! If I were staying here, I could be very tempted to keep you! But I'll have to see if I can find a good home for you, if your owner doesn't turn up. Here's your breakfast, and now I'm going to make myself a pot of tea and toast and take it back to bed. It's too early to get up yet!'

Her new companion ate, then disappeared out of the back door, but the toast was barely buttered before he reappeared. 'You've eaten my steak, you are not getting my toast! Besides, there's nothing worse than a dog who insists on being fed at the table. I'm not going to teach you bad manners!' The look of dolour made her laugh. 'You are incorrigible! No, you are not going upstairs again! That's out of bounds!' Congratulating herself, she shut the door to the stairs after her and carting her tray set it on the bedside table.

There was little joy in the breakfast while from downstairs she could hear plaintive whimpering. After finishing her toast and tea she could stand it no longer and dressed, then picked up her aunt's previous year's diary, remembering Aunt Jean had said they would give her a pattern to follow.

'High cloud. Easterly. Lifted rows two and three with West. Will again take up his offer to store and pack them in his number one shed. Perfect conditions and know they are safe.'

Amy reread the entry with mixed feelings. She needed a similar workplace but she didn't want to ask any favours of Dr Thornton. The thought reminded her of the phone. She pocketed it and walked down the drive, the pup running, looping and jumping beside, around and ahead of her. Each year's unsold bulbs had been planted on either side, gradually multiplying to cover the driveway paddocks. Thousands of yellowing leaves spotted the slopes.

Amy put the phone into the letterbox, and walked along the boundaries of her land. Apart from a few nut trees and three dozen old but laden apple trees higher up the hill, the grass was being grazed by sheep which belonged to Jonathon and Sue Thornton. Glancing along the line of the valley, Amy noted the changes since her last visit. Paddocks once grassed were striped with intensive production of flowers, mainly the russet, yellow, red and white of chrysanthemums, the 'gold flower' of the ancients. From the power and size of the equipment in some fields, West Thornton had found a goldmine. Her fields, apart from the daffodil ones, were the only ones left undeveloped on their side of the valley.

Back at the cottage, Amy noticed her companion had disappeared but she concluded he was resting in the sunshine in the back yard. She put on sunblock, adjusted her hat, went to the garage and drove to the daffodil area where she had been working the previous day. Following her aunt's map, she strung the pattern, checked the bulb numbers and began work. The ground was damp and she used a plastic bag over her sheepskin to kneel on. By eleven o'clock she had dug another row and packed away the bulbs, and she saw the pup reappear as she headed towards the kitchen.

'Yes, time for a change. My back aches. And we need food!' She patted the pup. 'We have to buy some—on my budget it won't be steak! Someone might be missing you. I'll report you to the council and Dogwatch. First, I'll have a shower and you can stay on guard outside and the door will be bolted!' The gleam in a pair of dark eyes danced in her mind. 'There'll be no Westleigh Thornton watching me this time!'

CHAPTER TWO

THREE hours later, Amy drove back to the cottage. 'Someone's taught you well! You deserve the new collar and lead. Next time, I will wear sneakers so I can run, too, when we stop at the beach.' She kicked off her high heels then began unpacking the groceries. 'The Dogwatch people were understanding, even when I said you were the loveliest, ugliest dog I'd seen. I told them your head and your paws are in proportion, but the rest of you doesn't match at all and they said you'd grow to fit. So you're a bit like me, I suppose. I was always the tallest, scrawniest girl in my class! Everyone tried to make me play goalie in basketball and I was hopeless. My co-ordination wasn't good. At fifteen, I was five feet ten, had braces on my teeth and boys used to call me the stick figure or else the metal skeleton.' She sighed with the past hurt. 'Gave me an inferiority complex the size of a mountain!' she finished, wiping out a cupboard and glancing down to see if the pup was chewing at his new play bone.

'My shoe! My high heels!' She dived after him, but he had the shoe in his grip and raced out of the door and up towards the orchard. As she came up to him he took off back to the cottage, the shoe like a talisman, hanging out his mouth.

'Drop it, you mad dog!' Amy's yell of indignation was hot air. She limped back to the cottage, reflecting that she had ruined her tights as well. The tooth-holed shoe lay on the kitchen floor, and she put it and its mate in the rubbish.

'The only high heels I brought with me! My budget is so stretched all ready, you wretched mutt!' She looked around but he had disappeared into the garden. Thinking he would turn up as soon as he figured he was no longer in disgrace, Amy continued stacking the supplies. She had always wanted a dog, but her parents had never allowed it, and while she was studying she had not been able to afford to keep one. Sighing, she recalled the council officer's regret that an ugly, large puppy's outlook was not long or bright.

'I won't let that happen!' she muttered.

The knocking on the open door surprised her and she smiled a greeting. 'Sue, come in. Would you like a cup of tea? Coffee?'

'Is the kettle on? Great! Tea, please. We've been searching for Jack O'Day. It suddenly occurred to me that he might have come across here. He used to call on your aunt regularly and regarded the land here like his own. Patrols every boundary! You haven't seen him? Silver hair? Bit rough, but he's good-hearted and harmless.'

'No.' Amy was relieved she hadn't met the local eccentric unwarned. 'But I have met your brother-in-law, West.' She poured the tea. 'Last night. In the daffodil field. He accused me of pinching bulbs and grabbed my keys; I suggested he was after them himself.' She smiled. 'Not the introduction of a lifetime! When he returned the keys, a little later, I was in the bath.' She saw Sue's smile and laughed, 'A foam one! I didn't think it funny at the time!'

'That explains the cat-got-the-mouse grin he was wearing last evening, when Jonathon told him you were here. West said he'd met you, then distracted us with trial plans we'd already agreed on, but I put it down to jet lag,' Sue chuckled. 'I should have guessed!

I work in the office for West, but after two I'm at home. The children arrive on the school bus at three-forty so the best time to call for a natter is between two and three. Any problems though, just pop over; between us, we'll see if we can assist.'

'My main problem is what to do for the best. The solicitor passed on an offer to buy the cottage. I want to keep some of the furniture but it all looks so right here. . .and then there's the packing and the garden, but first I have to deal with the special bulbs and the orders.'

'It's lovely in spring. West sold most of them for your aunt, but on daffodil Sunday Miss Radcliffe used to give bucketloads for a donation to a choice of four charities. With regard to the cottage, I know West wants to buy it and the land—he discussed it with us. It would suit us well; we can open a door and we've the whole area of the house. West can see that, with the children growing up, the extra space would be marvellous. Years ago, not having to build or rent let him put back the money into the business. Now, money grows on his trees, his flowers and his shops! He always admired Stone Cottage and the old trees.'

'Then my decision will affect you?' Amy's hazel eyes shadowed. 'I'm not certain that I want to sell. I feel as if I've come home.'

'It was your home when you were a baby, so that's natural.'

Amy looked round the kitchen. 'It needs redecoration.'

'Another question. You're the one who makes the decision. Sort out your goals, your priorities. If West doesn't buy the cottage, he'll build.' Sue checked her watch. 'I'll have to leave; come and have dinner with us tomorrow night?'

'I'd like that.' Amy waved Sue off, then returned to the kitchen and carried the dishes to the sink. Years earlier the stainless steel bench and sink had been installed, but the original frog on the lilypad taps remained. Her fingers smoothed the bulbous eyes as she raised it from the pad to release the water. The cottage might lack modern appliances, its 'parlour' was small, but its character resulted from the love of artisans. If she lived in it she would need a source of income. Aunt Jean had managed on an annuity and had supplemented it with sales of her special bulbs and flowers. Given time and money, Amy knew she could develop the orchard or the garden into profitable lines, but time and money were interdependent, her savings almost non-existent and Great-aunt Jean had left the cash in her account to Amy's sister and brother. Employment, temporary or not, was a necessity if she stayed and, with her training and experience as a landscape designer, the obvious person to ask was Dr Westleigh Thornton.

The image of West's laughing eyes taunted, and she pulled a face. West had built an industry, but he had started with land, money, expertise and skill plus relentless energy. If she sold she would be able to use the money to buy a flat near her family and work. Alternatively she could put some money into the flat, rent it out to pay the mortgage, and use the rest to seed her work as a designer, or she could return to life as a traveller for another couple of years. Touring was fun and there were many beautiful sights to see and interesting people to meet. . . But where else would be the sight of a tall, dark-haired man walking towards her, his outstretched arms full of creamy-pink roses?

'Good afternoon, Miss Radcliffe. My apology for embarrassing you.'

With West on the step below the door, she was on the same level as his eyes, noticing they were not black but deep, intense brown. Tiny white marks revealed laughter lines in the outdoors tan of his skin, and as she watched she saw the lines disappear and his eyes darken to dance. She admitted him with some reluctance, knowing he would have to put the roses down — there were too many to take from him.

'The roses are beautiful,' she murmured.

'A modern high health floribunda yet with the open heart of the old-fashioned rose. A favourite of mine.' West followed her into the room and let the roses cascade on to the table.

'A waterfall of roses!' Amy was awed by the beauty. 'The colour!'

'The colour of your skin flushed from the foam, Aphrodite.'

Thoughts of sexual fantasies and her attraction to the man by a bed of roses shocked her. She grasped at her everyday world. 'Vases! I'm not sure where they are. . .'

'Try the cupboard under the sink, and there's a splendid crystal one in the front room.'

'Would you fetch it?' Amy turned away and began filling the sink, adjusting the temperature to take the chill from the water. She plunged her hands into the water to cool herself, relieved West could not know her reaction. By the time he returned she had regained her composure and was calmly freeing some of the bunches before standing the blooms in the sink. Just as many were on the table. Selecting a dozen stems, she trimmed and positioned the blooms, enjoying their elegance in the crystal vase. She set it on the buffet where it was reflected in the antique mirror.

'Quite lovely,' West commented. 'The subtle colouring is a good match.'

Amy could see in the mirror too, where the open-necked blouse she wore revealed her warm flesh. Her throat blocked, West was making her feel like a teenager, unsure of herself. He wanted to make love with her. . .how did she know his thoughts? Could he feel her vulnerability?

'I wanted to surround you with them.'

Amy risked a glance at him, but meeting his gaze was a mistake; in his deep brown eyes were visions of herself dancing, shoulders bare, her body draped in gossamer and roses. She turned back to the sink and cooled her hands in the water of sanity; she was no dainty cherub but a sturdy, practical young woman. Placing more roses in another two vases did nothing to ease the sexual tension. She wished she could chatter inconsequentially, and stop the fantasies his presence had inspired. With an effort she remembered basic hospitality—he might leave if she offered refreshments.

'Would you care for a drink, Dr Thornton? I could make you some coffee or tea. I'm afraid I didn't think to buy anything alcoholic. There could be some here.'

'Would you like me to look? Aunt Jean and I often used to sit down to a whisky or a beer together.' He moved to the buffet and opened a small door. 'I'd like to hear you call me West.' He took out a whisky bottle, two crystal glasses and a jug.

Amy was aware of a surge of physical attraction as he walked to the sink, and the intimacy of standing side by side as he lifted the frog tap and rinsed and filled the jug with water. He washed the glasses with slow deliberation then with equal care wiped them dry.

'I always have loved beauty, Amy. These are more than a hundred years old. They belonged to your paternal grandmother. The one who gave you those green lights in your eyes.'

Amy ridiculed her own emotions. The man wanted her to sell him the cottage and the land. He had enough wit to realise that he had to change the disastrous first impression and he had selected flattery as his weapon and the abundance of roses as a gift. Once she responded, he would offer to buy the cottage and land.

'If I asked you to come to dinner with me tomorrow night, would you say yes, Amy?'

'No. I've already accepted a dinner invitation with Sue and Jonathon. It'll be interesting to get to know them a little more.'

'I'll get myself invited, too!' His laugh was a warm bubble as he held out the glass. 'I'll cook a meal for you another night.'

There was a pulse of sensuality as their fingers touched. Amy sipped at the fiery fluid, moistening her lips with her tongue, tasting the whisky, and was aware of his slow smile. It was almost as if he were already kissing her. . .making love to her. . .tasting the whisky on her skin. . . Appalled at her bacchanalian thoughts, she put the glass on the table and moved back to the cupboard where she had seen a large old crock.

'Temporarily I'll use this, until I can arrange the rest.' Carrying it to the sink, she filled it and piled in the remaining roses. Pain sliced at her left fingers and blood began to drip.

'Blast!' she grimaced, examining the slight cuts. 'I didn't notice the crock had a chip. It's nothing.'

'Have you had a tetanus shot?' West walked into the bathroom.

'Yes, of course.'

He returned with a long box with a childishly drawn red cross. 'Your work of art?'

'I was about seven when I sent that down one Christmas.' She tissued her fingers dry. West sorted through the contents and found a new box of padded plasters.

'I'll fix them on for you.' He studied the two cuts and applied the strips. 'Kiss better.' He brushed the back of her fingers lightly with his lips, but his eyes met hers. 'You should take more care of your hands, Amy. Fine things are worth attention.'

Fine? Her hands? They were long, capable and strong like the rest of her. Was he teasing her? As he packed away the first-aid box, she studied him covertly. He appeared sincere. Beside his, her hands had appeared slim and in proportion, although looking at them she could see scratches, and working she had broken several fingernails. 'I forgot my gardening gloves, but I bought some when I went into town.' She hesitated. 'Today's entry in aunt's diary from last year mentioned you helped her dig and store the bulbs. With all your enterprises that was kind of you. I'm sorry I accused you.'

'Friends help each other. I should have realised your identity. Proof that after a long flight my brain seems to function like a car running on three cylinders instead of four. You are welcome to the shed, either for packing or storing. What are your plans?'

'Originally I'd intended to send away the orders Aunt Jean had taken, keep a selection myself, sell you the cottage, and return to my work. Now I'm unsure just what I want to do.'

'Easy! Stay here. Days you can be surrounded with flowers, nights we can spend making love!'

'You're outrageous!' She needed the whisky.

'I told you I love beauty. The vision of you in your bath was glorious. You have a body made for lovemaking.'

'I'm not supposed to have a mind?' she said with sweet sarcasm. 'You must be the darling of the feminists, Dr Thornton.'

'Some roses have more prickles than others!' He beheaded the nearest rose and threw the petals towards her.

'They need them to lift themselves above the mess they would otherwise have to grow in!' Amy saw appreciation in his smile. She decided she liked his smile, the swift curve of his lips, the crinkle lines deepening and, in his eyes, laughter loitering.

'Tell me about yourself, Amy.'

A request. She considered it briefly. 'Potted history? I can't get away from gardens, can I? My family live in Auckland. I went to university, graduated Bachelor of Landscape Architecture. While I was at varsity I worked part-time with a local garden design company, went on to full-time work, saved like a miser, went overseas and blew the lot travelling. I worked in several gardens over there, came home two months ago and started work at my old firm.'

'You enjoy your work, Amy?'

'Yes, of course. I must be an earthwoman type, happy in a garden. The formal parterre style I can admire, but my preference is for the cottage garden, layers and a profusion of flowers. Perennials among shrubs, woodland with swathes of spring bulbs and orchard blossom, colour pictures tucked in unexpected corners. When I was a child I loved playing in the garden here. I'd pretend I was a flower fairy. I'd dance around the place, pirouetting and swooping—the

music was always so gloriously loud! Aunt Jean used
to play wonderful story music like the *Nutcracker Suite*
or *Sleeping Beauty*. Of course, I was very young. . .'
She saw the tender smile on West's face and did not
regret sharing her memory.

'You enjoy dancing? One night we'll dance till the
sun rises. There used to be a good band playing at one
of my favourite restaurants. Haven't been there for a
while, too busy to play.'

She was aware of his gaze on her mouth and sucked
back her lower lip. It was his turn to throw back the
whisky. She grabbed for a conversation line. 'Are you
still involved with research?'

'I try to spend three hours each day in the lab, one
or two hours in the fields and three or four on the
business side. But the times get extended. The
research team is small, but we add top students rec-
ommended by my professor in their holidays. It gives
them industrial experience and enables us to do more
experimental work. Two doing their doctorates this
year are working here most of the time and both want
to stay. My accountant disapproved but there are
advantages in being boss!'

'You like the business side, too?'

'Yes. I like to see the profit figures,' he chuckled.
'At heart, I'm a peasant. The soil and money! Sue
prepares the admin for me. It's on computer—we
designed a programme which follows the seed to the
market. She gets the daily and weekly reports from
the floriculture manager and he liaises with the farmers
when I'm not available. I have less to do with the
shops—they have their own staff—but I analyse the
monthly printouts. I spend more time studying the
trends from the florists and talking to the buyers. It's
vital to produce what the market wants.'

'How did you start? I recall Aunt Jean saying something about the traditional crops paying poorly and some of the locals having a struggle. Then ta-ra ta-ra ta-ra! You came home, a knight on a white horse charging to the rescue!'

West laughed. 'It wasn't quite as easy as that! There were a number of dragons to slay, prejudice, fear and incompetence. But I knew we had great soil in the valley, a microclimate suitable for growing flowers. I had worked on switching colour genes into plants which I knew were popular as cut flowers. Jonathon and I set up three hectares and planted it out. As well, I supplied plants to a few of the neighbours and I oversaw their work. Most figured they couldn't lose much and, as I pointed out, they had an example in Jean Radcliffe who had supported herself for years from daffodils. We were fortunate—the weather was good, the flowers bloomed and the florists went crazy over the new colours. They asked for our flowers. At the start I'd had to fight to get market space—no one wanted to bother with small amounts; the freight and air charges were excessive because I hadn't learnt to pre-order or bargain. Organising it took me nearly eighteen hours out of twenty-four. I scrambled from crisis to delays but I learned fast. When the season was over and the profits shared, I had more farmers wanting to join than we could supply.'

His story had kept the spotlight of his concentration from her and Amy wanted to keep it that way, and having worked in nurseries she was interested. 'And year two?'

'We knew we had to supply quality flowers on a regular basis. We set up a rotational plan to maximise growth and widened our range to lessen risk and then we built shade houses to extend the season. Basic floriculture. We had weeks of steady income, we could budget and we knew our target market.'

'It's grown from there.'

'Yes, gradually consolidating and experimenting over the years. Opening our own florist and nursery followed naturally. It's a multimillion dollar business. Everywhere I look there are opportunities. The permanent suppliers are my secret. Aunt Jean's advice again—find people who are good with the soil and pay them well.' He finished his whisky and shook his head when she offered the bottle. 'Are you trying to tempt me? You've done that already, Amy. No? It's time I left I'm expecting a couple of calls about our North American market trials.'

As he stood up beside her, Amy felt a *frisson* of satisfaction. He had to be six feet four. Even at five feet ten she would be able to wear high heels without worrying about damaging his ego!

'I'll see you tomorrow, Amy. I won't forget to put the phone in the letterbox on my way home.'

'Thank you.' Amy smiled as he put the crystal glass on the bench, then with a wave he was out of the door, closing it behind him. Her emotions swung up and down, riding a merry-go-round. West Thornton could be an entertaining companion, but his vibrantly male confidence was a challenge.

The scent of the roses prompted her and she spread vases around the lower rooms, enjoying the extravagant gesture. She carried three of the vases into the bathroom, placing them at each end and the centre of the dais, balancing their delicacy against the bath.

A whining and a scratching led her to the door and the pup eyed her hopefully. Her greeting was not enthusiastic. 'Villain! I meet a man who is taller than me and you ruin my only pair of high heels! Just my luck! And you go straight to the refrigerator!' She cut up some meat and he thumped his tail with total disregard for the music. 'I'm glad you're here,' she confided after he had given up on his plate-cleaning efforts. 'I have to collect the phone from the box and Sue said they were looking for someone called Jack O'Day. Who knows how many other characters visited Aunt Jean? I'm not as brave as I look. Come with me?'

The puppy accompanied her with much meandering and sniffing to investigate the night delights of the grassy edges of the drive. Safely back inside, phone beside her, Amy sat to read and the puppy settled himself in a rug by her feet. Her fingers curled in his wiry hair. 'Whoever dumped you did me a favour. I wasn't sure I could manage on my own, but with you here I feel safe!' She smiled. 'At least, I do when West Thornton isn't with me.'

Before she went to bed Amy showed the pup to his mat in the laundry, but in the morning he was settled on the foot of her bed. His start to the dawning day was instantaneous and Amy, getting up to let him out, decided to begin work too. As she dug and collected the bulbs, she noted cars arriving at the packing sheds, work beginning in the flower fields and the departure of the truck for the market.

It was a long muscle-wearying day, and by the time she put away her forks Amy had completed two-thirds of the digging. She stored the bulbs in the garage, locking her car outside. Again she bolted her door before running her bath, choosing *The Magic Flute* for her entertainment. Soaking in the bath, she studied her hands; they had improved with the creaming and massaging and by trimming the nails. The echo of

West's words 'fine things are worth attention' had been a reprimand.

Why she should care what West thought of her was a puzzle. At twenty-four she was through with dreams of finding a handsome, rich man who would sweep her off her feet. She smiled sourly—even the idea was close to a physical impossibility. Anyone attempting to sweep her would need a very big broom! The concept of home and family of her own one day was very strong, and she had already considered the list of qualities she wanted in her man; thoughtfulness, a sense of humour, a steady disposition, a generous nature and an ability to love. It didn't seem an impossible list but often she had found men selfish, arrogant and lazy. West was not lazy, and seemed unselfish, but there was more than a touch of arrogance and pride in the man.

Her thoughts turned to her friend Jason, whom she had met overseas; he was returning to New Zealand and his letters had suggested a closer relationship. Amy wasn't receptive to the idea even if he more than fitted her list. A horticulturalist, he was practical, his letter more comic than romantic. She couldn't imagine Jason ever giving her a hundred roses the colour of her body! Nor could she see herself dancing in the garden with him in semi-nude splendour, whereas West would revel in such a romp. . .

Toeing the dragon tap to release more hot water, she lay back chuckling at the image, accompanied by the lush richness of *The Magic Flute*. Jason had enjoyed heavy metal, and his habit of switching her radio to the stations he liked had been a wellspring of irritation. With their separation she realised that he had been a symbol of home. She didn't love him. In her next letter she would tell him how she felt. Her

earlier dithering through not wanting to hurt him
seemed muddleheaded.

To the magic music of the flute she levered herself
out of the bath and stepped on to the platform, the
roses, warmed by the humidity, scenting the room.

What to wear was not a problem. Thinking it was
unlikely she would be going out, she had included her
black dress trousers and a cream silk blouse, just in
case. One of the rosebuds she set in a wave of her long
hair before rolling it smoothly into a pleat and fasten-
ing it with a favourite old-fashioned comb. The flower
was a softening touch to an otherwise severe line. With
her hair up, she decided, she looked presentable even
if her comfortable black driving shoes were scarcely
the accessory she would have chosen.

She hooked her coat around her shoulders. The
evening was balmy, but by the time she was ready to
return home she would need the warmth. A final spray
of perfume and she set off down the stairs. The puppy
looked hopeful.

'You've had tea! Sorry, my friend, but Jonathon and
Sue have dogs. I'd better lock you inside, there are
guard dogs next door at night, and they'd make
mincemeat out of a lumpy, bumpy puppy.'

Amy pocketed the key and walked down the driveway singing 'Pa-pa, Pa-pa, Pa-pa, Papagena!', *The
Magic Flute* in her mind. There were definite advantages, she decided in living in the country and one was
being able to sing at full voice without others hearing!

'Pa-pa, Pa-pa, Pa-pa, Papageno!' a baritone joined
in.

Spinning round, she saw West, and as he
approached she enjoyed his sensual, rich voice. It was
natural to sing with him and at the end of the verse
they both chuckled.

'Dream woman! She not only has a body made for love but a voice of a bellbird!' West's eyes made light of his words. 'Good evening, elegant Amy. *The Magic Flute* tonight while you relaxed?'

'One of my favourites. Aunt Jean maintained it was too sentimental but she had four different records of it and a disc!'

'I always liked the birdman, Papageno. He's not the prince but a credible man, wanting love. He makes mistakes, but he learns and provides humour.'

'And he wins his Papagena at the end! Do you know more?'

'That's about the only song I can sing right through. May be the profundity of the lyrics!'

Laughing, they reached the farmhouse and West went to his own wing to shower and change. Without him, everything seemed flat and dark; even the moon hid behind a cloud.

CHAPTER THREE

SUE met Amy at the door and introduced her to the three children before excusing herself for the last preparations.

'We've had our tea,' the five-year-old informed her, 'but will you save me a chocolate? Uncle West always does, but he might have to go looking for Jack again.'

'You're not meant to ask guests to give you their chocolates. And Jack O'Day never goes far.' His seven-year-old sister indignantly smoothed the pin-tucks on her pyjama-front.

'Dad and Uncle West were out looking for him till midnight,' the eldest, Marty, dark-haired and dark-eyed like his uncle explained. 'You should have heard Uncle West tearing into him this morning. Poor Jack! Uncle West said he'd lock him up all day today.'

Amy was horrified. That anyone should have such an inhumane attitude to an elderly person, possibly suffering from Alzheimer's, appalled her. 'Surely not!' Her words were sharp.

'No. Uncle West's really a softie.' The girl grinned, showing gaps of two front teeth. 'Jack met us after school. He was fine.'

Not reassured, Amy's thoughts were scattered as Jonathon walked into the room, pointed to the clock and kissed the children goodnight. The three snail-paced to their bedroom. Jonathon poured her a drink as Sue returned.

'Apologies for being a hopeless hostess, regardless of what the magazines try to convince us we should be

38

able to do! I've invited West and a couple on the other boundary.' Sue handed out a tray of delectable, artistic nibbles. 'Kerryanne and Arnold Webster are orchardists, and Kerryanne is our local drama producer; she's a wonderful organiser. Arnold's a distant relative, was at the local school and then boarding school with Jonathon and West. All good friends!' Sue stood at the sound of a car pulling up at the portico. 'Right on cue! Kerryanne knows her entrances. Excuse me.'

Amy was introduced to the couple as they entered. Arnold tall, muscular and bronzed, was a similar type to his friend Jonathon, and Kerryanne was a bubbling person, with her own sense of theatre, voluptuously pregnant, spreading herself on the couch, announcing she had done so many prenatal exercises that she would be likely to produce the infant after dinner. As no one seemed alarmed by the information, Amy relaxed until, five minutes later, West entered the room. Aware of his smile, she found it difficult to keep in front of her mind the new, shocking knowledge. Avoiding West, she carried on talking to Arnold.

West placed himself beside Kerryanne, giving her a kiss at the same time. 'How's the baby, lucky lady?'

Amy was surprised by the jealousy that spurted through her. Arnold was so devoted he expected admiration for his wife from other men! Over the excellent dinner, Amy found West's dark eyes watching her but, with Kerryanne's stories entertaining them, it was possible to avoid conversation with him. After the meal they moved into the living-room, but to Amy's relief West excused himself and left.

Without West, Amy enjoyed the lively conversation, the stories of people in the valleys, and she could supply anecdotes from her aunt's letters. When it was time to go Kerryanne and Arnold offered her a lift home, but she told them she needed the walk after the excellent meal and wine. After thanking her hosts, she slipped on her coat and walked down the drive and out to the road. Once away from the house she was dismayed by the absence of the lighting; used to the street-lights of the city, she had not thought to carry a torch. Grateful for the moonlight, she walked along the side of the road, and her senses adjusted so that she saw a hedgehog snuffling in the bushes, the sound-less flight of an owl over a field, and the reticent movements of the tops of the trees in the shelter belts. Enjoying the tranquillity, the harmonic music of the night, she missed a step, realising the shadow by her gate was a man. Fear painted a dozen pictures.

The whistle of Papageno's theme from *The Magic Flute* relieved her. West met her as she walked towards the gate. 'You gave me a fright!' Amy accused.

'I've been looking for Jack. A whistle carries further than a voice and I didn't want to alarm you. I'll walk you to the cottage. Something's been annoying me, so I'm glad of the chance to talk. Before dinner I had the impression that we were friends, I went home to shower and change, and fifteen minutes later you gave me the ice-bucket treatment. Why?'

'Jack O'Day?' Amy stopped to pick up the phone from the mailbox. 'That's why you left? Has he gone missing again? Why didn't you ask us to help search?'

'Arnold has Kerryanne to worry about and Jonathon stayed up last night with me, hunting for him. It isn't fair to ask him again.'

'I think you're quite wrong. The hills could take a search party. At least it's not a cold night. I'll go home and get a torch and help you. Who's responsible for him?'

'I am of course.'

'Then I don't approve of your lack of care. Shutting him in for half a day is reprehensible!'

'There are times when it is necessary.'

'You are unbelievable!'

'I don't understand you. Some customers can't stand him. Personally I feel they have a problem, but I respect their right.'

Amy wished she didn't have to fumble for the doorlock. 'You put your customers before him! Such a terrible, frightening experience! You both need help, counselling. . .' About to add more, she was startled by thumps from inside the cottage.

'Wait!' West put his hand on her arm. 'Someone's inside. Get down, out of sight. Dial Jonathon, then the police.'

Before she could explain he had thrown back the door and snapped on the light. A beach ball rolled on the floor.

'It's the puppy!' Amy kicked the ball. 'I'd locked him in. Come on, fellow!' The sound of tail-thumping led them both upstairs and she switched on the bedroom light. Lying on her old-fashioned single bed was the golden-eyed puppy, his tail giving the ecstatic drum roll.

'Jack O'Day!' West exclaimed. 'What are you doing here?'

'This is Jack?' Amy couldn't stop the bubble of laughter and relief erupting into a full fountain. 'That's so funny!' She dropped back on the bed, gasping for breath, the puppy giving enthusiastic support. Her fingers entwined round his collar as she patted him. 'You're Jack!' Again mirth shook her, but seeing West's anger she attempted to compose herself.

'You dare lecture me on animal rights when we've spent the last nights looking for that blighter!'

West's accusation only made her laugh again.

'You attempted to steal a valuable animal! Jack! Get off that bed!' he roared.

The dog sidled off and stood looking adoringly up at his master. West ran downstairs. Amy realised he was about to leave and she owed him an apology and an explanation.

'Wait! Please!' She went to the refrigerator but Jack was already there ahead of her. She knew West watched as she bought out large chunks of gravy beef. 'I guess if I'd been up till midnight looking for him, I'd be annoyed too. But no one mentioned a dog. I was asked to watch out for Jack O'Day, silver hair, a bit rough but a harmless wanderer in the habit of visiting here. I thought he was a local Alzheimer's patient who needed care. That's why I was so upset when the children talked about you shutting him up. It didn't fit the good things I knew of you. As for stealing Jack, that's ridiculous! I reported him to the council and Dogwatch.' She went to the cupboard and found a suitable container, inserted the meat and then washed her hands. 'Take this, I bought it for him. There's also a lead and a couple of toys.' She pictured him playing. 'I'm sorry. I don't know much about dogs.' Her hands were fondling Jack's soft ears. 'He's all feet and head. I know he's just a mutt, but I think he's beautiful, and he's such good company—I wasn't scared at night with him here.'

'Stop making me feel such a ratbag,' West groaned. 'Tomorrow I might smile! The sight of you on that bed, seductive with laughter, was too much!' He slammed the meat back into the refrigerator. 'Jack can continue to spend the next few nights here with you. If you want to borrow him, that is.'

'I don't know what to say.' Amy, sensing his frustration, was cautious. She grabbed at Jack. 'I will look after him. Although he has a habit of racing off in the mornings!'

'He comes to be fed. Although he might look starved, I monitor his diet exactly. According to the book he's actually a fraction overweight; let him finish the meat tomorrow and, after that I'll resume feeding him.' He thrust his hand through his hair. 'And don't let him sleep on your bed!'

'No, of course not!' Honesty pricked under West's glance. 'At least, he starts off in the laundry on his mat, but he wakes me up licking my toes in the morning.'

'Half his luck!' West's tired eyes lifted. 'Tonight, shut the door. Remember, he will grow into a very big dog. I will share my bed with the right woman but not a dog!'

'Yes, West.' Her arm already around Jack's cuddly neck, she smiled. 'If you want to borrow my car, you can.'

'I'll walk, I need to cool down.'

His eyes left her in no doubt as to his feelings and she was glad to remember the bonbons in her pocket. 'Would you pass these on to the children?'

'They conned you too! I'll pass them on in the morning. Goodnight, Amy, Jack.'

He shut the door and Amy clicked the bolt into place. Jack padded after her but she shut him into the laundry. After half an hour of piteous scratching and whimpering she compromised and made his bed up on the hallway between the two bedrooms. It seemed to meet his approval.

Amy sectioned off the box and placed the last of the special bulbs inside. The field looked as if it had been decorated with five brown medals and stripes where she had dug. Ahead would be the chore of checking each bulb, selecting the best to pack up and courier to her aunt's customers. Amy, easing her tired body, had found the first week's efforts at the cottage hard work, but with the special bulbs dug and work begun on the rose garden, she knew she had made every daylight hour count. Even if she did sell to West, she wanted to hand over the cottage and garden in good order. She played with the thought, and looked around the fields and back at the cottage, seeing what she could do if she had time and money. The woodland area and the copper beech were already magnificent but she would plant more, then reset the herbaceous borders, set steps down from the cottage towards West's boundary, remove the old fence which separated the side paddock from the driveway field—the impossibility of removing thousands of daffodils to the woodland area stopped her plans.

Her shoulders protested as she sat on the grass and bent to wipe down the forks. She wasn't sure if she could summon energy to walk with West and Jack O'Day along the beach. Honesty compelled her to admit she would crawl with broken legs if West asked her. The man was fascinating. They could talk about so many things—plants, parks, gardens, trees, birds and of course music. She was grateful that Aunt Jean had said they were to split the collection. The task had meant West had to spend time with her as they sorted the tapes and records and discs. Already he had spent three evenings at the cottage and they had enjoyed discovering their favourite operas, discussing various performances they had both seen, and then there had been the joy of finding in the bottom shelves early recordings of famous singers of the past. The previous evening they had been laughing, talking and listening hours had seemed minutes. She hadn't wanted West to say goodnight.

A bumble bee swaying like a bungee jumper on a long-stemmed white clover flowerhead made her smile. Absorbed, she lay on the grass watching it, and when Jack O'Day reappeared she reached out and patted him. 'Hello, my darling Jack. Now, don't you trouble that fat bumble bee, he's been giving me such entertainment. Have you had a good day? I have too, but my back aches so much. . .pity you don't go in for massages—it's just what I need.'

'I could offer!'

West's voice startled her and she turned to see him, and mentally groaned at his devastating sexuality. Hair damp, body summer-hard, muscles glistening under the shirt he had closed with one button, shorts resting across his hips.

'Look—clean hands. I've just had a shower.'

Amy struggled to sound rational. 'I didn't hear you.'

'Sneakers are well named!' He dropped down beside her 'Lie down again, I'll help you relax.'

The prospect of having the pain eased encouraged her to roll over. Kneeling beside her, he spread his hands over her shoulders and she sighed with pleasure as he began kneading away the strains of the week. When his hands slipped under her T-shirt and undid her brassiere, she stiffened but did not deny him—the restriction had irked. Under his hands, curving and massaging, her tenseness began to melt.

'That's so good,' she murmured soporifically after some minutes. 'Just carry on forever!'

'Forever's just a little long!' West moved his hands slowly and rhythmically. 'Besides, those two pain knots in your neck and lower back have shifted; you'll feel better now. Too much digging and stooping in one week.' He leaned forward, kissed the centre of her shoulder blades and pulled her T-shirt down. 'You're a little country mouse working away at dawn.'

'Jack wakes me. And time is limited.' Shifting to her side, Amy smiled at him. 'I took three weeks from work, but if I ask for more time off they may decide they could let me go. Design work is hard to find. I couldn't afford to be out of work.'

'The sale of the bulbs would compensate.'

'The bulbs? No. They are precious because each one represents so much work from hybridisation on. But to sell them won't bring much. Bulbs sell for peanuts!' She looked at West. He was smiling, shaking his head. 'Am I wrong?'

'Yes, my beautiful, smooth-skinned woman! They are prizes, every one. How do you think your aunt afforded all her visits to see you? Her overseas trips? Her music? The annuity paid for roughly three months' living expenses; the bulbs did the rest.'

'And the pension for all over sixty-five,' Amy reminded him.

'Take a good look at her books. In the desk. I helped her with her tax for years. If you don't mind work, you'd earn as much here.'

'I haven't my aunt's passion for hybridising. Besides, I enjoy my work, planning and redesigning domestic gardens.'

'We haven't a landscape service in the firm. I could put you on the books with a retainer. The sketches you showed me were excellent.'

'You're serious?' She looked at him and saw sincerity. 'Then I could stay? West, I could kiss you!'

'Promises, promises!' His dark eyes were alight with humour.

Amy was conscious that their physical attraction was like a rope being slowly pulled taut. More strain and a rope would either pull them together or break. She wasn't ready for either.

It was difficult to regather the conversation with West's eyes searching her face. She plucked a seed-head and shook out the seeds. 'West, if I stay, you won't be able to buy the cottage.'

'There are other possibilities.' He eased back on to the grass beside her, his eyes on the sky.

Amy, trying not to react to his closeness, saw he was watching the flight of a bird, an eagle gliding on an updraught. 'Yes, Sue said you could build on the farmland.' She shivered as the eagle dived.

'I could move in with you. Mutual benefits.'

Amy felt her breath quicken. With his last statement, West had invaded her space. She tried to move back but his arm drew her closer. 'No, don't deny it, there is attraction between us.'

She nodded, not risking speech. Her heart drummed.

'You have lips that I find enticing.' West spoke softly. 'Your lower lip is slightly over-full, as though it longs for kisses.'

Amy did not want to resist. She closed her eyes as he touched her lips with his own, warm, firm and moist. The kiss deepened as he intensified the tender exploration, seeking and finding responses which freed the dam of desire. Amy was trembling as he dropped kisses on her cheek, her ear, and nuzzled her earlobe.

'Sensational, my Amy!'

His breath tortured her as he lifted her hair and kissed sensitive spots on her neck and she murmured as he took her mouth, her lips already hungry for him. She felt her breasts swell and ripen to his caress and her body's fevered anxiety for his touch. Her hands were delighting in the tactile pleasure of holding and searching him, his loose shirt allowing her to enjoy the clean-washed, male freshness with its overlayer of citrus and musk and his torso firmed by years of physical effort. Kisses an intoxication, clothes an imprisoning restriction, her fingers scrabbled at his belt. His chuckle and easing away hit her like a shower of cold water.

'Amy, do you think we might move into the bedroom? Or if you particularly like the texture of mother earth, at least let's move behind the cottage where we can't be seen by anyone who might happen to drive past!'

Shocked and dismayed by her sexual response, Amy put her hand over her mouth, her eyes widening as she saw her own disarray. Pulling down her T-shirt, she adjusted her bra, aware of West's gaze.

'Don't look!' she growled indignantly.

'Sweet Amy, of course I'm looking. Your body's magnificent, smooth, curvaceous and perfectly proportioned. When we lie together we're just the right size for each other. The attraction between us is explosive.' He reached out a hand and stroked her thigh.

'Please don't!' Her voice wobbled, revealing that he only had to touch her to restart the throbbing ache.

'Why not, Amy?'

'It's not right, is it? You don't love me, it's just sex.'

'Just sex? It's about the most powerful force there is between two people. It unites, divides, destroys, conquers. The urge to procreate is a basic need.' He deliberately stroked her again. 'And it feels great.'

With determination she pushed his hand away. 'It's also dangerous, and is highly over-rated!'

'This comment from the woman who was trying to rip my shorts off me a minute ago!'

'I was not!' she blustered, but on meeting West's smile she shook her head. 'I can't understand my reactions. I hardly know you!'

'My dear Miss Radcliffe, we've practically grown up together.' West's lips twitched. 'Your letters were entertaining—Aunt Jean read out sections. Unfortunately, she censored the romantic parts!'

'I have to disillusion you. Apart from one disaster when I was seventeen, I haven't had a great love affair.'

West sat up and pulled her into the circle of his arm. 'Tell me,' he prompted.

'I fell in love with a football hero, and he was so much in love with himself I didn't realise he couldn't spare any for me. He wore me as an accessory. The crash came when I wore new high heels and someone jeered because he wasn't as tall as his partner. That was it. End of affair. It just about destroyed me, because I'd convinced myself he loved me. My self-esteem dropped to ant level.'

'He broke your trust.' West held her with comfort. 'I'm sorry, Amy.'

'After that, I retreated to study. Gradually I came to terms with what had happened and worked out my own philosophy. No sex unless I was sure I loved. Few really tempted me. Except for Jason.' Her eyes lowered. 'And you! Please do up your belt. This is so embarrassing!'

He leaned forward and kissed her. 'I'm flattered. Where's Jason?' West made a charade of looking for him as though expecting a sudden appearance.

She smiled. 'Yes, Jason would be almost as big as you! He was in London on a working holiday, we met in the gardens at Kew. We had a lot in common. He's a horticulturalist and he'd read of Aunt Jean's hybridisation work. . . I wanted to love him, I want so much to be loved, to have a family. It seems such a simple thing—to grow with someone, to have children——' she shrugged her shoulders '—but our time off rarely coincided and there were always others around, and no privacy. We used to joke about it, but I think neither of us was sure enough of our feelings to make a commitment. We'd talked about a tramping holiday together, but when I had the letter from Aunt Jean that she had only a few weeks left, I caught the first plane back. Jason was unimportant, Aunt Jean meant so much. I'm glad we had the time together.'

'Now she's brought you home.' West patted her back soothingly as Amy wiped her still earth-marked hand across her wet eyes. 'Come on, you've just put a streak of mud across that lovely face. We'll go inside and I'll make you a drink and a meal while you have your bath. If you're insistent, I shall leave the door half closed.'

'If you're nice, I shall get all weepy again.'

'I have broad shoulders!' His smile kissed her. 'I'll give you a hand to stack and store these bulbs.'

The task steadied Amy, and together they put the bulbs in the garage. In the cottage, West forestalled her shower by running her bath while she was upstairs selecting clean clothes. The strain of *Die Fledermaus* caused her to smile, appreciating West's choice. As she passed through the kitchen again, she saw West washing potatoes.

'If you're longer than half an hour, I'll come and fetch you!' he teased.

She slipped into the bathroom, added bubble bath as a precaution, adjusted the water, eased off her clothes and climbed into the giant bath. There wasn't quite as much water as she liked, so she kept the taps running while the overture played. After scrubbing her skin clean, she lay back, her head just above the water, eyes closed, relaxing with the music.

Roses, splash-landing in front of her, made her glance up.

'Perfect!' West was at the door, his eyes studying the meeting of foam and skin. 'You look so erotic with your shoulders laced with foam.'

'Out!' She scooped a handful of water, then realised the movement titillated him further. 'Something's burning!'

'Me!' he laughed, but he disappeared to reappear a moment later. 'Dust on the back element. Do you eat carrots and yams?'

'Yes.'

'I can't see a lot to make dessert. Fruit and some cheese?'

'You're taking advantage!'

'Of course.' He sobered. 'Seeing you in that bath, surrounded by roses, is one of the visions which will remain with me. Know that you are beautiful.'

He closed the door as he went to the kitchen, but Amy was too disturbed to enjoy her bath. She needed time to recognise her own emotions. Hastily she dried and dressed, returning to her bedroom to blowdry her hair. The night air was cooler and, remembering his shirt and shorts, she carried down a large jersey. On her it was oversized but it would fit West, and if he wore it the jersey would cover the sensual strength of his upper body. She cringed, remembering how eagerly she had explored him, as though the locked store of her sexuality had been dynamited open by his touch.

It was warm in the kitchen as he had lit the old stove, and she dropped the jersey on to the day-bed, avoiding contact. 'In case you're cold.' Then seeing his expression she grasped for conversation. 'You're very domesticated—the table set, the rose by my serviette, the food waiting to be served.'

'Work as a kitchen boy, then assistant chef while I was at varsity,' he laughed. 'Cleaning up is the chore!'

She slipped into her seat as he held it ready, then he poured a sparkling wine into her glass. 'This is for Aphrodite, *Methode Champenoise*, Marlborough's finest. I laid in a case for Aunt Jean five years ago and there are several bottles left. To the woman in the bath!' he toasted.

'To the man who gave me a hundred roses!' she smiled.

The meal was superb, and Amy relaxed, enjoying the food, the music, the wine, the pleasure of being with West. At the table they lingered, together they cleared the dishes, stacking them on the bench. They were standing side by side when the dance scene opened, and West bowed formally and, deftly removing the cutlery from her hands, swept her round the floor. It was impossible to dance in sneakers and, laughing, they stopped, their bodies close.

In character with the opera, West raised her hand and kissed it, then kissed each finger and, turning her hand, he opened her palm and pressed butterfly kisses along her arm, her breast, her neck and then her mouth. She was trembling, aching for him and she recognised her own need as well as his. Meeting his kiss with her own, she moaned as he began undoing her blouse, caressing her shoulders, finding erotic spots she hadn't known. His eyes, black with passion, sought her consent and she struggled with her decision.

'It's all right, my sweet Amy, we'll take it as fast or as slowly as you want,' West murmured, his voice rough, 'but sex is going to be so good for both of us.'

Sex, not love. The same mistake she had made earlier, but this time there was no pretence of love. Drawing in a breath, she pushed him back. 'West, I can't handle a casual affair.'

'I don't think I want that, either.' He filled two more glasses and gave her one. 'In fact, I'm astounding myself by thinking along permanent lines. Marriage.'

'Marriage!' The word warranted a healthy gulp of wine.

'Yes. Isn't it obvious that we are well suited? We've only to look and we want each other.'

'Sex is not a reason for marriage!' she spluttered.

'It's a good foundation. But we've so much more! Look, my field is genetics, an old pun, my sweet. The soil has been in our families for generations. You love the earth. I've watched you, there's an innate harmony you have with the land. We understand each other's work and appreciate it. I've never met any other young woman with whom I could discuss plant genetics, opera and beauty! We come from similar religious and cultural backgrounds, physically we are alike, our body structures, long, lean and strong. Our senses are in tune, so we have the sexual force between us. It unites us in spite of ourselves—you attract me and *vice versa*. As a breeding pair we're a match!'

'You make us sound like a pair of rabbits!' she protested.

'Not discriminating enough!' he laughed, and his fingers lifted her hair, finding the sensitive spots around her ear. 'These last few evenings we've both enjoyed. Yet they were simple pleasures, walking Jack O'Day, listening to music, finding out our likes and dislikes. I realised I'd gone too fast for you at the beginning and I've had to force myself to give you time to trust me. You know I've been wanting to touch you, to kiss you, to make love to you.'

Amy trembled as he traced the outline of her lips with his fingers.

"The last few nights, Amy, I found it very difficult to leave you. Since you entered my life, my research, my enterprises are not enough. I need you, my woman. Together, we can make each other happy. Later on, when we're ready, we'll marry and have a family.'

Amy, struggling against the desire his fingers exposed, knew there was a question she had to ask. 'West, there's rather an important ingredient missing. Love?'

CHAPTER FOUR

'LOVE? To be truthful, Amy, we're better off without it. This way we can rationalise everything, trust each other, without wayward emotions cluttering up the scene.'

'That sounds cynical. You've had more experience of it than I have?' Amy felt chilled, defeated.

'In my past.' He led her over to the old couch. 'My first girl was special. Kerryanne. We met at varsity. We thought we loved each other, but it was attraction and opportunity and young hormones colliding. Everyone said we were crazy, and the more they said it, the more determined we became to make it work. We were together nearly four years. All expected us to marry, but the longer it went on, the more I knew we were living a farce. The crunch came when Kerryanne wanted children. I couldn't agree. I wanted my kids born into a stable, caring home and Kerryanne and I had nothing left holding us except the glue of guilt. At that stage I was barely earning enough to support us, although I was working almost round the clock.' He thrust his hand through his hair. 'There was an opportunity which had to be followed up. Instead of giving it to an agent, I decided to go myself. It gave me a break, some rest, and time to rethink. I saw sense and wrote to Kerryanne. Arnold called the night she received my letter. He often used to visit but I never realised he was in love with her. Because he's a stalwart friend, he hadn't said anything. Within six months they married. Now, they have two children and expecting number three!'

'They were at Sue and Jonathon's dinner party.' Amy remembered the intimacy between West and Kerryanne and the prick of jealousy.

'Yes. They're lucky with each other, living happily ever after.' West was wry. 'I went out with other women but it was a long time before I risked love again. On holiday in Australia, I saw Melissa. I fell totally. We had a tempestuous love affair, both of us blown off our feet. Crazy. Then I found out she was married and had two little boys at home in Sydney. I was devastated. I would have fought hundreds for Melissa, but I couldn't hurt children.' He was silent for a moment. 'The experience seared. Celibacy developed into a lifestyle. My anger and grief for our loss shut me off from the attraction of women, I buried myself in my work and the harder I pushed my energy, resources and experience, the more I achieved. Seeing you in your bath shocked me into realising success at work wasn't enough.' His eyes teased, but he dropped his voice to its lowest note, 'Aphrodite.'

'I'm not. . .' Her words were kissed away as he drew her into his arms, his hands working their magic as his lips enticed and caressed. Shivers spasmed through her.

'Protected?' The skin round his dark eyes crinkled. 'I'd like to make you pregnant, my sensuous Amy! Think of the fun we could have! First a Papagena for me, then a Papageno for you, then a Papagena for me, then a Papageno for you, my Papagena!' He puckered his lips and gave her a noisy, smacking kiss.

Amy looked at him sideways, unsurprised to find him glancing back at her the same way. 'Children!'

'Like a flock of chickens around you, my Pa-pa-pa-pa-gena!'

She looked at him and loved him, his warmth, his humour and his cherishing tenderness. 'Be serious! And please. . .stop that. . .this minute,' she gasped, as he stroked a sensitive spot. Her limbs seemed to melt as sugar caramelised under heat.

'Amy, if I don't stop now, you might end up pregnant!' He rolled off, then kissed her fingertips which had been exploring his body. 'No condoms and I bet you haven't any either!' His self-mocking smile twisted his lips. 'I didn't intend this to go so far, so fast. I'm frustrated and you are too, but I want you to think about this without cursing me for an irresponsible idiot while I'm away.'

'You're leaving?' Disappointment choked her voice.

'Only nine days. A delivery run to our staff at Sydney, Brisbane and Singapore. It's important to check everything is being received in good order and to find trends in the market. My schedule will be tight, but I'll think of you every time I see roses. I leave early in the morning.' Light switched on in his eyes. 'Come with me! You must have a current passport and I can arrange an extra ticket. While I'm busy during the day you can see some of the gardens, or go shopping. Money, I can give you. The nights can be ours!'

Amy did not dare look at him. Her body told her to go but her mind waved red flags; when it suited him, she was to be a satisfying diversion he was prepared to pay for handsomely. The knowledge grated.

'No?'

She bent her head, avoiding his gaze. His touch was a feather breath on the back of her neck and it sent thrills down her entire body. She felt him turn her

head and his lips pressured hers as she bent back, until
she was supported by the ridge of the couch. His kisses
became urgent and hungry, his lips covering her abdomen, his hands finding her erogenous zones as her
willpower faded.

'You can't resist me, my Aphrodite.' His eyes were
black with passion. 'You want me as much as I want
you!'

Amy nodded, acknowledging the truth, and despair
shadowed her face. Was she to be trapped again by
her own sexuality? He was not offering love! 'No,
West. I can't go with you. The bulbs. . .the orders. . .'

It wasn't a brave excuse but it was one West
appreciated. She felt him release her.

'Of course, Amy. I'm sorry, desire overruled judgement.' He thrust his fingers through his dark hair in a
gesture of control, struggling to smile. 'Not a word
about hitting below the belt!' He moved to the buffet
as though he had to keep a physical distance between
them. 'While I'm away, write to your boss and give
him notice. Also, think about the cottage. If you want
to retain the ownership, that's fine. I'll move in with
you, my sweet, but I'll pay for the alterations. An
architect whose work I admire has specialised in keeping the traditional character yet adding sympathetic
space. Dishwasher behind a rimu cabinet to match the
rest of the kitchen, and so on. The bath on its pedestal
and the taps stay! I'd like a covered swimming-pool,
sauna and spa, and of course we'll have to add on
more bedrooms for our infants, and I'm sure you've
some ideas about the living area, and the garden.' He
pulled a paper from the shelf and pencilled a number.
'The architect's phone—phone! Organise that, will
you? Have the fax from my flat transferred here.'
Again he was scribbling a note. 'An authority in case

the phone company question it. Any expenses just
send to my office. Am I going too fast for you?'

'No, I love the thrill of being run over by an express
train.'

'It's all your fault for being such a sexy creature!'

She could see the intensity of need as he looked at
her. Instinctively she clasped her hands across her
breasts. She swallowed. It was too much; the man
could warm her just by looking at her!

'Sex between us is natural, my Amy.' He spoke
softly, reassuringly. 'I'm just as stormtossed. I'm getting out of here while my resolution holds.'

Amy felt the quick kiss, then he opened the door. A
joyful barking told her that Jack O'Day had been
waiting outside. She watched as West jogged across
the daffodil paddock and disappeared behind the protective shelter of the hedge. Suddenly drained of
energy, she had to lean against the door for support.

Three days of uncertainty and longing helped her to
decide. The time had given her a chance to face her
own emotions and she knew that she had fallen in love
with West, but there was little consolation in the
thought. Love hurt because she knew West did not
love her. He was open in his desire for her, he liked
her, he enjoyed talking to her, but his heart was
Melissa's. Amy tugged despairingly at the dockweed
and then reached for the garden fork. About to wreak
vengeance on the weed, she paused, noticing the tiny
plant of bleeding heart beside it. Gently she worked
the trowel around the dock and eased it out, leaving
the bleeding heart intact and with room to grow.
Watering it and paddling the soil with a little fertiliser
was the best she could do, but the finding of the plant
had brightened her thoughts. If she was strong and

refused to allow West to move in, perhaps like a delicate plant their love would grow.

Collecting the mail, she was surprised to see an unfamiliar letter. One glance and her heart raced, knowing it had to be West's writing, strong, artistic and decisive.

My dear, seductive Amy,

The pilot has just informed us that we are flying at so many thousand feet, so therefore I am very close to heaven at this moment—it doesn't feel like it. There is a rather spoilt youngster throwing up in the seat in front, and the odour is scarcely pleasant. There is, however, a hostess who has brown hair almost, but not exactly, your colour. When she turns round I am disappointed, because, although she has an attractive face, it's not your face with your expressive eyes. I can see your lower lip curving into a tantalising, kissable smile as you read this letter.

Already I grow—impatient. (What were you thinking, you sexy wench?)

Have my bed shifted up to the cottage. I remember the single beds your respected great-aunt had in both the bedrooms. Old cast-iron originals which may do our infants in time, but not for us, my long, leggy woman, which reminds me, I kiss your grubby earth-stained knees. Or have you taken your long, lingering bath? In which case, I kiss those graceful shoulders.

West.

The letter made her remember just how forceful and persuasive West could be. She had arranged a telephone for herself and ignored West's commands about the fax machine, and she had every intention of ignoring his request for the bed. Her smile widened at the thought of West's bed being drawn along the road to her cottage and the interest and speculation of the neighbours!

The next day she saw the mailcar stop again and raced down the drive, Jack O'Day barking beside her.

Dear addictive Amy
My hotel suite has a very large bed and half of it is wasted. I am lying here thinking lecherous, lustful thoughts of a lovely woman in her bath. . . I will have to stop—my body can only give/take so much!
Business has been good. One potential trouble spot has been sorted out, another avoided. When we are lying together in bed one night, I'll tell you about it. You see, it won't be all sex!
West.

She reread the letter and felt her cheeks pinken and knew it was nothing to do with exercise. Writing back was not an option as he had not given her an address, and she did not want to ask Sue for his itinerary. Instead she drove down to the beach with Jack O'Day and ran along the sands, hiding the letter in her pocket. The following night she had another letter to add to the collection.

My dear Amy
It would be good to talk to you. If you had the telephone on, I could ring you and whisper suggestions in your ears. Just had a crazy vision of you in the buff wearing a telephone over each shoulder. . . Why do we say she/he has the phone on? But then again, I do have my mobile phone in my pocket when I'm in the fields! I'm slightly high on duty-free whisky and loneliness for you. Singapore tomorrow.
West.

Jack O'Day was already at the letter-box when the mailcar stopped in the morning, and from her corner of the garden Amy called him back. It was a blow to find no letter from West, but she was not empty-handed. A letter from Jason readdressed from her home showed how deeply her feelings had swung.

Jason's letter was brief, detailing his plans for his arrival and suggesting a meeting in Auckland. She frowned, realising their letters had crossed. Returning to her weeding, she attacked the corner with such vigour that by teatime she had a pile for composting that threatened the rest of the kitchen garden.

The next morning, a familiar airmail envelope sent a surge of joy through her, and studying the postmark she knew West had not forgotten, the delay had been due to time zones and the distance he had travelled.

My own sweet dove, Papagena

My rep here has a small bird in a cage, but no magic bells. Did you fly into Singapore on your travels, Amy? Wonderful city, the shopping is amazing, but I am too much of a country bumpkin to do more than marvel, and then rejoice that I live in a green valley with only a cottage and a couple of farmhouses in sight.

Another chain is interested in a weekly order but I will have to do further work to see if we can meet the demand. The potential is huge but I have seen damage done in the past by giving a commitment recklessly.

I have been very conscious of you, so much that at times I expect you to walk in and smile. . .and then I am bereft.

West.

Amy felt a warm glow thrill through her as she read the letter. Floating back to the cottage, she saw the grass was greener, the trees more lush, the late roses blooming more magnificently than they had five minutes before. She wanted to sing, to dance, and she ran inside to put on *The Magic Flute*. Papageno's entrance where he claimed to have killed the dragon and saved the prince was hardly the start to romance, but then her first encounter with West had not been well favoured either!

As she drifted round making some lunch, she wished for the twentieth time that she had asked West at what hour he would be returning. The previous day she had been to town and purchased extra food, but her resources were limited. It was a considerable saving that the vegetable garden although neglected, had continued to grow. An extravagance had been the hand-carved Panpipes she had bought from a street artist, but having sighted them she had to buy them for her Papageno. In the evening she had tried to play birdsong notes and been rewarded when a bellbird had flown to investigate. Jack O'Day, barking vociferously, had shown his disgust at the visitor, but a word and he had settled.

Finishing her salad, Amy wished Sue and Jonathon had mentioned West's arrival time. Two days earlier she had entertained the family for tea and enjoyed the occasion, and Jonathon had dropped in the conversation that West would ring them from his Auckland flower farm with details of his flight. It had been difficult to refrain from offering to pick him up at the airport. Explaining that she had decided to stay, at least until the following season, had been greeted with approval which, Amy decided, proved how kind they

were, considering that her decision meant they would
not have the extra space from West's flat.

As the daylight gave way to dusk, Amy finished
work and took a shower. For once she left the music
off, as she wanted to hear the arrival of West's car or
Jack's excited barking. After spending a long time
washing, drying and curling her hair, she dressed in
her evening trousers and pretty blouse, wishing she
had more clothes with her. With an apron on, she
checked the casserole she had made. If West was to
arrive, he might appreciate the meal. As it grew dark
she lit the candles, switching on only the side-light so
the room would look romantic. Two hours later she
put the food and cutlery away, her anticipation and
appetite soured. She put Faust on the compact disc
player, the mood heightening her melancholy. It was
after midnight when she patted Jack at his position by
the landing, and retired to bed.

Sleep eluded her as she tried a variety of scenarios
which could explain his absence. At half-past two she
reread his letters and then threw them and the symbol
of love, the red rose into the rubbish. She tossed and
turned and, half an hour later, retrieved the letters
and the broken rose and put them into the dark
recesses of the wardrobe.

It seemed no time at all before Jack woke her and
she went downstairs, sleepily opened the door for him
and, yawning, went back to bed. Dreams of giant
gastropods herded by Jack, muddled with impressions
of letters surrounded by red roses, then she was
dreaming of West, hearing his deep voice whisper her
name. She smiled as he told her she was beautiful, his
hands caressing, enjoying the sensation of his touch on
her hair and face. She nestled against the warmth and
firmness of his body and the faint citrus tang of his

aftershave. . . Her eyes flew open—no dream had ever been so real! West kissed them closed.

'Good morning, sweet Amy.'

His voice was a warm, deep chuckle.

'West! What are you doing?'

'Kissing you! What I'd like to be doing should be penetratingly obvious.' His eyes held mocking tenderness. 'Sweet Amy, you were so irresistible asleep, your hair drifting over the pillow. An invitation I couldn't deny.' He moved on to his side, then looked at her, his smile twisted. 'How do you sleep in this bed? It's terrible!'

'It's quite comfortable for one.'

'We need my bed.'

'You ordered me to get it. Not even a please! Can you see me going to your brother and asking him to load your bed on the trailer? Imagine it being carted along the road!'

'A Brueghel scene!' he chuckled. 'Jonathon and Sue will be happy for us.'

'But how long would we be happy, West?'

'You want the "happy ever after into the sunset" ending?'

'Yes!' She was conscious she had disappointed him as he swung round to sit on the side of the bed. 'In one of your letters you mentioned how easy and how damaging it was to give a commitment recklessly. Because we are so sexually attuned, it's hard for us to see the hazards.'

'Nail up a yellow and black road sign: "Slacken speed. Heartbreak ahead"?' West ruffled her hair. 'Amy, that's one thing we won't have to worry about. None of that gut-tearing emotion. Thanks to Melissa, I'm out of the range of Cupid's nasty little arrows. As far as I can see, the only danger would be to you.'

'What would happen if I fell in love?'

'I'd castrate the man concerned!' he grinned. 'So I'm revealing myself as selfish and macho as any other male!'

'What if Melissa came back into your life?'

'A hypothetical question. The situation won't arise. Melissa lives in a different country, she has a husband and two sons. It's history.'

Amy shifted uneasily, but her movement attracted his attention and she pulled the sheet up to her neckline. West bent forward, peeled back the sheet and kissed her nearest shoulder. The touch sent a spasm through her and West's mouth curved and kissed her.

'I also wrote about kissing that shoulder!' He was teasing again, smiling. 'You are enticing, sleep-rumpled.'

Amy fought against the pleasure. If she were to begin her campaign to win West, allowing him sex without his love was not in her rules. 'I'd better get up.' She glanced at the clock. 'It's late.'

'It's raining, you can't work outside. But it's not like you to be a slug-a-bed!'

'I stayed up late last night, hoping you'd come,' she admitted, a little shy of revealing the depth of her emotion to him.

'I was looking forward to seeing you, but when we drove up the road I noticed there were no lights on. It was after ten so I thought you'd gone to bed. Neither Jonathon nor Sue said anything about my move here and my gear was at the flat.'

'I decided you weren't going to move in.' She eyed him, then softened. 'But I ached to see you. I've never known such a long day. I used candles because they hid the shabbiness of the room, and I pulled the curtains to keep the heat in.'

'My romantic Amy!'

West leaned over and kissed her mouth, and desire warmed her. Aware of her response, she made an effort. 'You are the king of romance. Your letters! I enjoyed them!'

'A bit of fun. But I did miss you. I felt better when I wrote to you.' He kissed her forehead, her cheeks, her chin and then her mouth. Amy, her limbs languorous, resisted his magic with a gasp of will. 'How did you get into the cottage? Have you got a key?'

'No, but I know where your aunt used to hide one. It's probably still there, unless you've shifted it. The door was wide open. Jack was guarding it, but he allowed me in!'

'I was so tired this morning. When I let him out, I must have left it open.'

'You must take better care, my woman. I should move up here, just to protect you!' He began caressing her breasts. 'Some villain might find you in your bed and seduce you,' he murmured deep-voiced, and moved to kiss the sensuous spots at the base of her throat.

'With Jack around?' Amy protested, pushing West away. 'Would you stop that! You're taking advantage!'

'With you, my Amy, I intend to take every advantage I can!'

'And Great-aunt Jean thought you had high principles!' Her voice was muffled by his thick, dark hair. West's hands explored further, tantalising and delighting. From the corner of her eye she saw Jack sidle in and look at her, knowing the rule about dogs in the bedroom. Amy nodded for him to jump on to the bed.

West muttered, 'Aunt Jean would have——'

Jack's enthusiastic barking as he leaped on top of them to join in the fun provided the old bed with too much weight. With a vibrating crash the end fell off, and all three, in a tangle of blanket, sheets and limbs, slid to the floor. Jack, yelping, recovered to speed downstairs; Amy, reduced to an hysterical heap of laughter, could not be sympathetic as West thumped the wall.

'That should teach you to take Aunt Jean's name in vain,' she bubbled, as she made an effort to stand. She saw his wry grin break through his frustration. 'That was so funny! You looked so astonished! No wonder I love you!'

'You. . .love. . .me?' West whitened under his outdoor tan. He spoke the words so quietly her laughter ceased. She looked away, wishing she could take back the words.

'Is it so bad?' Her voice sounded strained, her throat full of stones.

'Yes. Without emotional blackmail we could have had fun and supported each other. Love makes you vulnerable.'

'And that is wrong?' The tears were pricking behind her eyes.

'Of course, it's wrong! You offer me your ecstacy, your dreams, your happiness. I cannot accept. I have nothing to give you.'

Amy held her head straight as West ran down the stairs, and she heard the kitchen door slam as he left. Somehow she gathered the crushed plant that had been her dream and put it aside. One day in the future, when the thought was less painful, she would toss it out and think of what could have grown. Her cheeks were wet as she saw the rain dribbling down the windows and the grey of the sky. Everything was a mess, from the untidy room with its broken bed to her own life with her splintered hopes.

Sniffling back to recovery, she remembered the passion in West's eyes. Only a man who was capable of great love would have reacted with the emotion he had revealed. If love had hurt him so badly, couldn't love also heal? The thought encouraged her to dress, and she picked up the bedding, set it on a chair, rolled the feather mattress into a pile, and examined the broken bed. The iron frame had snapped above the shaped section which slotted into the end, a break which could be hard if not impossible to fix. Grateful her methodical aunt had tied the bed's spanner to it with a cord, she took the rest of the bed to pieces and set it up against the wall in her aunt's former room. She struggled to get the other bed apart. It took time, but by dint of using boxes to hold one end while she wrestled with the other, she managed to reassemble it in her own room. She wished she could fix her relationship with West as quickly, and the tears started down her cheeks again. While she kept her thoughts away from him she could control her emotions, so to stay busy she began to prepare the bulb order and check the figures.

Downstairs she searched her aunt's book for the addresses of the customers. Having found the annotated list, Amy worked her way through, jotting down prices. After an hour she knew West had been right, the amount was considerable, but most had sent payment which had already been credited to her aunt's account. There was little cash outstanding. As she pored over the previous year's records, Amy grimly noted the amounts required for specialised packing containers and courier postage. In her own account she didn't have sufficient left to pay the costs. West had offered work but she was reluctant to go to him and admit the problem.

If she stayed, would her presence be unfair to West? Love had conquered him just as it had almost destroyed her. The thought caused a sob to rise and the tears to drip. Jack whining eagerly, signalled a friend's approach. Hurriedly, she blew her nose but the mirror by the buffet reflected pudgy, red-rimmed eyes and untidy hair. She combed it back into place and picked up her sunglasses at the familiar knock.

'West!'

'I'm sorry. I left rather abruptly. I came to give you a hand fixing the beds.'

Amy twitched as he reached forward and removed the glasses. 'Blast you, West! Can't you leave me some dignity?'

'That's one thing you never lack, Amy. Don't try to hide from me. I hurt you, but I believe in what I said.' He gestured to the stairs. 'I'll take a look at the bed.'

'It needs a blacksmith. Don't worry, I swapped them over.'

'On your own?'

'Jack wasn't a great deal of help.' Her mouth curved but her smile died as West deliberately looked away. She stiffened at the rejection and moved back to the safety of the papers.

'Knowing Aunt Jean, everything would be in order——' his tone was businesslike '—but if there is any difficulty, I may be able to help.'

It was her opportunity to explain, but pride kept her silent.

'My work has been piling up too, so I should get back to it.' He bent and rubbed Jack O'Day. 'You stayed here today, Jack?'

'My fault, I——' her heart was pounding, '—should have taken him to you. . .'

'I'm sure he was a comfort.' West was brusque. 'Thank you for feeding and exercising him. I have a small gift for you, but I'll drop it in some time.'

Amy shut the door after he left, and the tears sped down her face. 'Jack, how am I going to bear it? Just seeing him makes me want to nestle against him, but he's so formal. He knows I'm in pain, too. I'm turning into a modern wonder, a portable waterfall!' She blew her nose, and looked out the window as the rain started again. 'Even the weather is miserable, Jack. I can't take you out now, seven men with seven hoses are pumping the rain down.' She moved back to the table and added the sums again, but the answer had not lessened. 'I'll have to sell something, but what?' she murmured to Jack. 'Apart from the cottage, all I have is bulbs—thousands of them. I'll sell some bulbs!' Examining the idea, she knew that desperation had inspired the answer. 'Jack, if I made them up into packets of five and ten, and take them from one corner, I'd earn enough to keep me for a few months and cover costs. I would lose the sale of their flowers in the spring, but by then I should have gained some landscaping work. With or without West!'

Amy checked previous figures and mapped out ready sellers from her aunt's daffodil plan. The rain continued to fall and Jack seemed little interested in the prospect of a walk. As the night darkened, she carried on identifying the bulbs and checking purchasers who could be interested in a special offer. At midnight the sight of Jack prowling round the kitchen made her realise his discomfort. She opened the door and he shot outside. When he didn't return a few minutes later, she switched on the outside light.

'Jack! Come!' Silence worried her. She threw on her coat and shoes and picked up the torch. Heavy cloud hid the half-moon so the countryside was dark. The beam of her torch lit a strip, making everything else a sea of blackness. She whistled but Jack did not respond, and she guessed he had hared up to his favourite walk among the apple trees where he would be hogging down windfalls.

Reluctantly she began walking up the hill. The ground was greasy and she searched her steps with the torch, cursing Jack's sudden disobedience. Reaching the orchard, she hesitated. The trees looked like demented, accusing, forest ghosts. Jack was not there. Annoyance gave way to concern and her fears doubled when she remembered that a farmer in the next valley, after having trouble with a sheepkilling dog, had threatened to shoot any dog straying on his property. The possibility terrified her.

She would have to ring West and tell him. The thought was not pleasant but there was no choice. Amy risked running but, after a fall which covered her with mud, she slowed. Drizzle gave way to rain, the lights of the cottage seemed further away. Stopping to whistle and call for Jack, she heard West answer from the direction of the boundary hedge.

'Amy? Is that you? What on earth are you doing?'

The wide beam of a torch gave her his position and she ran towards him, then slithered on her own diggings which had turned into rivulets of mud. She could have howled with anger and fear but she was too busy spitting out mud and struggling to stand.

'West, it's Jack! I've lost him! I should have taken him for a walk earlier, but it was so wet. . .' Amy was babbling, but a friendly bark turned her to relief, then rage. 'You wretch! I've been up and down that hill looking for you.'

'He heard me locking up and came over.' West steadied her. 'Don't ever take such a risk again, Amy. It's crazy to walk on the hills in this weather. And at this time!'

'I kept remembering the farmer's threat.' They had reached the cottage door and she opened it with wet hands.

'Jack always stays this side of the hill. You need a hot bath and a drink and this fellow needs a rubdown. I'll take him home with me.'

West stood in the doorway, but Jack was already in the kitchen and he proceeded to shake himself, spraying a fountain of raindrops over the floor. 'Jack!' she protested, then glanced down at her own garments. 'I look as if I've been mud-wrestling.' She dropped her coat and shoes in the laundry and grabbed an old towel to rub Jack. In front of West she was suddenly aware of the effect of her wet T-shirt and leggings. The sexual tension between them was like a blue-white flame being blown towards paper. One move and she would be in his arms making love. But afterwards he would leave, and she would be desolate.

CHAPTER FIVE

'You need a hot shower and a drink.' West moved to plug in the kettle but his voice was gruff. 'Jack can wait, he's barely damp. I'll leave him with you, if you like.'

'Thank you.' She continued to rub Jack O'Day, but her shivers were catching up with her.

'Amy! Go and have a shower, right now!' West loomed over her and she was afraid he would hear the thundering of her heart. His look of exasperation and frustration followed her into the bathroom and she closed the door and leaned against it, gaining her breath before switching on the shower.

Showered, hair washed, she dried and put on her towelling wrap, tying it into place. In the kitchen Jack had stretched himself before the stove and was already dry. The kettle had boiled and a mug was placed ready beside it. A note with the single word 'Goodnight' was under the mug. She went to the door and locked it, took her drink and went upstairs, put on warm nightwear and climbed into bed, too exhausted to think of the miseries of the day.

The morning showed red, orange and purple banners in the sunrise sky and Amy, letting Jack outside, decided it was likely to be another wet day. Her first priority was to send away the orders, but that meant a trip to town to purchase as many of the courier pouches and boxes as she could afford. The mail arrived on her way out and her worries increased when she received the letter and rates demand from the solicitor's office. She needed work, but after West's rejection she wouldn't approach him.

Dressing with care, she drove into town and went to the employment office. The only work on offer was apple-picking and she accepted a few week's work with reluctance. The money would solve several problems.

On her way to the car she saw a Victorian-style wallpaper in one of the décor shops and stopped to admire it, realising it would look beautiful in her bedroom. She pulled a face, thinking the whole cottage needed refurbishing, but the first area to tackle had to be the kitchen-living area where she spent most of the time. It was ridiculous to enter the shop when her funds were so low, but inside the pressure increased when she saw the perfect paper for the kitchen and was told only a few rolls were available. Even if she did the redecorating, the cost of the materials could not be contemplated, but she asked the shopkeeper if she could put it aside and used her grocery money for the deposit. Walking to the mailshop, she purchased the bulb boxes and stopped at the mall for milk and bread, mentally promising herself many apples from her trees.

Rain slashed at her windscreen as she drove home, and for once they did not stop at the beach for a run. Instead she drove to the flower farm to drop off Jack O'Day. On other mornings she had taken Jack to the gate and one of the pickers would meet them and take him to Sue or West. Because of the weather she used the formal entrance for the first time and, unfamiliar with the office building, Amy had impressions of space and light. Before she had time to identify the painting on the wall Jack, tugging at his lead, whined excitedly as West opened a door and walked towards them. She let go of Jack's lead and wished she could launch herself at West, just as sure of his love.

'Good morning, Amy.' West bent down to stroke Jack. 'No ill effects from your midnight stroll?'

'He seems fine.'

'I meant you, Amy. Going to town?'

'I've been.' She felt awkward, trapped by the wish to talk with him and anxiety to leave. She gestured to the surroundings. 'This is quite a place.'

'It's a good work environment. I'll give you a conducted tour some time, Amy.'

A dismissal. She turned to go, feeling large and inadequate. Jack's damp nose and his silky hair against her hand was an immediate comfort. West's action in stepping forward to open the door while he restrained Jack made Amy move with brisk steps to the car. She was shaking as she drove down the driveway, her vulnerability to West contrasting with his detachment.

Concentrating on driving, she didn't stop until she reached the road running to the beach, and she wondered why she had instinctively gone there.

It was the same beach where she had run several times with Jack O'Day, but then the waves had been darting playthings tagging the sandy shore, scampering back to play hide-and-seek with the rocks. At that time her relationship with West had been on a similar teasing level. Since then there had been dramatic changes. Her placid nature had been retuned so she was affected by every nuance in the way West stood, the movements he made, his speech, even the things he did not say. The grey sea matched her forlorn mood. Waves rolled forward to smash themselves open, revealing their green torrents and white foam against the unyielding black rocks. Was her love to be similarly self-destructive?

West needed love as much as anyone and his emotions could surprise him. Tides did turn. Encouraged, Amy realised that if she was starting apple-picking the next day she should make use of the time left. In a happier mood she drove home and began assembling the boxes for the larger numbers of bulbs. Working in the garage, she wrote labels and began packing the orders.

Daylight had faded into a sullen grey sky before she returned to the cottage, but she couldn't eat. Instead she began preparing more boxes until a familiar scratching and whining at the door announced Jack. West was walking towards the gate, and at the sight of him she had to catch her breath and fight the desire to run to him.

'Good evening, Amy. I'm just going to give Jack a walk. It's stopped raining but the hillsides will be slippery so I thought we'd go along the beach. Care to come?'

Amy's usually deft fingers became sausages as she continued to shape a box. 'I don't think. . .' Jack, woofling at the pompom on her slippers, gave her a golden-eyed, pleading gaze. 'I'll get my coat.' She ran upstairs and pulled on her windjacket, hat and sneakers. Part of her rejoiced that West had liked their evening walks and wanted them to continue; a more sobering reason told her he was polite because he wanted her land and cottage.

'Busy?'

'Yes, West, I've a job picking apples for a month starting tomorrow, so I've been packing bulbs as fast as I can. The boxes are simple enough but I thought I'd do a few dozen tonight.'

'Picking apples? I thought you were going to work for me.'

'I didn't think it would be a good idea, in the circumstances.' She locked the door and pocketed the key, glad that the activity deflected the intensity of West's dark eyes. Eyes which saw everything.

'My wagon's at the office.'

Amy walked beside him to the gate by the hedge. As she passed the sign about dogs she turned to West. 'I was sure I heard dogs baying the first evening. I was too scared to come after you.'

'A tape recording. Set off by heat sensors. If you had gone further it would have triggered a phone at the homestead and at the security agency. They have dogs with their patrols but they are well trained, they wouldn't utter a bark unless necessary. Our fellow could learn from them!'

Outside the main block she saw his late model four-wheel-drive wagon. West opened the door for her and Amy settled in the luxurious seat and reached for her seatbelt. Jack jumped up into the rear. West stopped the wagon facing the sea. The wind of the morning had dropped, the sea had rolled to a sulky pouting silver. She released Jack and he ran helter-skelter along the shore line, barking madly at seagulls slow to flap off, leaping at them as if he expected to take off after them.

Jogging together they headed towards the curve of the beach and, after thirty minutes, returned. It was a simple outing yet, as they drove back to the cottage in the deepening night, Amy was already treasuring the moments of companionship.

'I'm glad you came along, Amy.' West was concentrating on steering up the rutted drive. 'This morning, seeing you threw me. I had been worrying about you, wondering what to do for the best. I'd made up my mind to keep the situation cool, to let distance grow between us. As you left, I saw the pain in you, and I felt as if I'd taken a rosebud and crushed it.' He pulled the vehicle to a stop and switched off the engine. 'Honesty of emotion at this level is hard for me, Amy. I'm probably not putting this well. I was trying to avoid hurting you. The fact that you're prepared to pick apples instead of asking me for work stunned me.'

'I've picked apples in England. It's only for a few weeks and will pay for the courier boxes and the rates. Design work can take a lot of advertising and preparation before work comes in.'

'True, but that's not the real reason, is it?'

'I didn't want to ask you for anything,' Amy admitted.

'Do you want me to stay away? I can usually insulate myself and my work from disturbances, but today I kept thinking of you. I could have sent one of the staff over with Jack, but I wanted to see you. I'd like to continue our friendship. But I'm aware of your emotional involvement and the cost to you.'

'You're asking me if I can accept friendship instead of love?' Amy struggled for rationality. 'The starving man is not going to quibble if offered dessert instead of a main.'

'Do you want me to continue bringing Jack O'Day?'

'Of course I want Jack. Except it's not really fair on you. He's your dog.'

'Perhaps you'd rather have a dog of your own? I'd happily buy you one.'

'I'd love to have a dog, but the chances of finding another Jack O'Day would be millions to one. Besides, until I'm established, I can't really afford the vet bills and registration let alone the food. I watched Sue and the children feed him a couple of times; he's got the hunger of a hippopotamus!' She patted the silver neck and head which reached over her shoulder. 'And he still looks a lumpy, bumpy puppy! West, he's growing every day. He's bigger than most of the dogs I've seen.'

'A full-grown Irish wolfhound is a large, powerful dog, Amy.' West smiled. 'Our Jack is the son of champions!'

'I've been an ignoramus, Jack. Calling you a mutt! And you with a pedigree that goes back generations!' It was natural to slip in a Gaelic lilt to her voice.

West laughed. 'You do that well!'

Amy saw his gaze go to her mouth and knew he wanted to kiss her. Sexually she attracted him. Before she had told him of her love he would have kissed her. Pain swiped her as he jerked open his door. Before he could walk round to her side, she climbed down and went to open the cottage. Released, Jack ran to inspect his water dish and the back garden. West remained by the wagon.

'I'll say goodnight, Amy.'

She heard the coolness of control in his tone. 'Goodnight, West.' She called the words, unwilling to turn to face him, tears wobbling on her eyelids. Dashing them away, she entered the kitchen.

'Amy, I can't leave you like this.'

West had guessed her hurt and followed her. She tried to speak but her throat was clogged. She swallowed. 'I'm fine.'

'As fine as the weather yesterday.' West pushed back her hat. 'I don't like to see you cry.'

'I'm not crying!'

'No, of course not! You've just invented a new way to wash those beautiful green-lit eyes.'

His gentleness gave her the courage to look up. She

saw the tenderness in his expression and again hope flared.

'Look, Amy, you probably don't feel like cooking, but you should eat if you're going apple-picking tomorrow. It's hard work. Come with me to a restaurant; you'll have a good meal and I'll have an independent opinion on the plants there. Our branch in town supplies and arranges them but I like to check the standard is being maintained. Having an excuse to eat out is half the fun!' He looked at the clock, 'I'll pick you up in a little over an hour. I have to see Kerryanne and Arnold, then go home, shower and change.'

'Has anyone suggested that you have a dictatorial attitude sometimes?'

'I made you smile again!'

'I should make up the boxes.'

'Leave them. I'll get the staff to do them for you, on the next wet day.'

'Thank you, but I can manage.'

'You're as stubborn and independent as your great-aunt!'

'Are you sure you want to invite me for a meal?'

'It seemed like a good idea a few minutes ago,' he smiled. 'I enjoy being with you.'

She would have gone through the valley of fire without the magic flute for such an admission, she mused while she was showering. But she was no delicate Pamina but a sturdy Papagena, and the man she wanted was not looking for love.

Looking through her wardrobe, a little later, she wished she had something different to wear instead of her dress trousers and blouse, but she was grateful that her mother had couriered down another pair of high heels. She tied a silk scarf on her shoulders and checked in the mirror. The bright carmine red of the silk suited her colouring and, after a search of cosmetic counters, she had found an exact match in lipstick. She flicked through her few pairs of earrings but decided against them; none was the right colour or mood for the occasion.

Amy smiled when she saw West. He was wearing a dark suit and a silk tie which included the vibrant colour of her scarf.

'Perfect match!' chuckled West. 'And I know you haven't seen this tie before. I bought it in Singapore.' He looked at her. 'You are beautiful, Amy.'

Amy drew in her breath with pleasure. West's compliment was sincere. Beside him she did not feel a gawky giraffe.

'I bought you a present for looking after Jack O'Day, walking him every day and so on, while I was away.' West handed her a tiny box. 'I brought it over for you the first morning, but I forgot it.'

Amy undid the paper wrappings with the care they deserved. Opening the box, she saw the sparkle of two large ruby earrings set in gold. 'West! They're magnificent! Such a marvellous colour!'

'I'm glad to hear you say that. The colour attracted me. A deep red for a ruby. I remembered you wearing a lipstick in rich carmine red, the one you are wearing tonight. Put them on.'

Amy hesitated. 'I don't know if I can accept such an expensive gift. . .'

'Compared with what you offered me, it's nothing,' West said quietly and then smiled. 'They won't suit me! And considering the time I took to find the colour I wanted for you, the least you can do is accept them.'

Amy gave up her protest, pushed them into place

and enjoyed their sparkle in the light. 'West, they're wonderful!'

'The colour is yours.' West looked smug. 'Let's go, I'm a hungry man.'

The restaurant was one Amy had noticed before. An old shop, it had been altered to allow the diners a view of the spotlit garden along one side and, despite the lateness of the season, there were some flowers blooming. Inside a floor-to-ceiling pole had been set with descending discs and each supported a basket of plants, ferns or impatiens in full flower.

'It's lovely! A fountain of flowers!' Amy admired.

'The owner is a friend, so I wanted something special. Depending on the season we have pansies and violas, begonias and so on. Incidentally, I notice you looking at the style of the place. It was converted by the architect I mentioned.'

'I'm impressed. But I won't be able to have anything done to the cottage for a long time. Unless I start picking golden apples from my trees!' she chuckled. 'I'd love to build a big conservatory off the living area of the kitchen.'

'Sounds like a good idea. The front parlour is hardly used. It was built to face the road, not the sun.'

The arrival of the owner and the introductions which followed made her forget the cottage and financial concerns. The meal was superb, from the local mussels poached in wine to the bowl of late strawberries. Conversation was relaxed but Amy was aware of an underlying tension between them. She could see West ignoring the beat of the dance band, but Amy, determined to treasure the evening, would not allow the disappointment of not dancing to spoil the occasion. She toyed with a strawberry, biting its luscious ripeness with epicurean delight. West, putting his right hand to his face, screening his eyes from her, made her look at him questioningly.

'For my sake, Amy, would you stop eating those blasted strawberries in such an erotic way! Come and dance!'

She had longed for the invitation, but from West's expression it was the lesser of two evils. The music had a quick beat and she slipped into step opposite him, patterning his steps. Dancing was a joy for her, and as the band played she could see West ease his shoulders, and the rest of his frame relax in the pleasure of the music and movement. The switch in the beat followed smoothly and she moved into his arms. The slow, languorous mood suited her emotions and she nestled against West, enjoying the tactile pleasure of the fine wool in his suit, the firm structure of his body, the way she could rest her head against his shoulder, the close weave of the threads in his fine cotton shirt. She closed her eyes to savour the moment, the clean, warm smell of him, woody, faintly citrus, sensually appealing, the music bonding them, melding their movements so perfectly that as it drew to a close they were as one. She felt West's kiss on her hair, but then the music stopped.

It was like ice-water being poured over her as West disengaged himself. Looking at him she saw the quick pucker of his mouth.

'Amy. This is too difficult.'

'I could have danced with you forever!' She regretted the words as soon as spoken. She tried to lighten the intensity. 'Usually I'm too tall, but the music——'

'Amy!' West cut in. 'It's not going to work, is it? Both of us have tried to be "friends" this evening but the sexuality between us is too strong.'

Looking at the fierceness of his expression, Amy struggled to remain calm. 'Why are you so angry?'

'Isn't it obvious? I want to have sex with you. You deserve more, Amy. Someone who takes advantage of another's love is a form of life on a level with a grass grub.'

'Maybe science will discover a good side to the grass grub.'

'Amy, we're leaving. There's a limit to my good intentions and I've reached it. I'll keep out of your way in future.'

Minutes later they were driving back along the country road, the sound of the sea loud in the silence between them. As they turned into the side road which led to the homestead and the cottage, Amy ached for her loss. From being on top of the ferris wheel with its vista of happiness she had been brought speedily to the base and tipped unceremoniously out.

The headlights caught the letter box, revealing its sagging lid and broken flap.

'You should replace that box. And get a few truck-loads of gravel for this drive.' West's anger was in his voice as they lurched towards the cottage. Amy was hurt by his attack but she was determined not to show it.

'You're right. Aunt Jean told me she intended to have it done this summer. I've other priorities. The drive doesn't worry me, it's a challenge, a slalom course avoiding the potholes. In this vehicle, you don't even have to be a good driver.'

West's eyes were glints in the shadow of his face as he stopped the vehicle. Amy didn't wait for him to move round to open her door. She jumped down and pulled out the large, old-fashioned key from her bag.

'That would give a burglar open sesame, Amy. It's pathetic!'

'Stop criticising! Why are you doing this to me? Spoiling our golden evening!' Crushed by his attack, she looked at him. When he would not meet her eyes, Amy was chilled. 'You want to fight with me.' Unlocking the door, she scarcely noticed Jack O'Day's affectionate greeting. 'It's all right, West. Perhaps it would be best if you kept Jack O'Day. With apple-picking I'll be working late, I won't be able to take him for walks. Thank you for letting me have his company so long. It is appreciated.'

Wordlessly, West walked out of the cottage and Jack trotted along beside him, nestling his head in West's left hand. It was a comfort gesture and Amy closed the door on the sight, feeling alone and abandoned. She heard the vehicle start and saw the headlights light the drive. A gasp of pain broke from her but she refused to allow tears. If West was so frightened of her love that he had tried to force an argument to break their relationship, he had the problem.

Amy reached for the fine clips to release the ruby earrings. As they lay in her hands she admired their colour and sparkle. In the restaurant she had enjoyed being with West yet, when they danced, she had felt his tenderness and desire like a warm cloak.

Could she have imagined the unity, the completeness of those few moments? Was it possible that West did love her but did not know his own emotions? What was real? The letters, the rubies, his tenderness, his understanding? Would she ever know his love?

CHAPTER SIX

AMY reached out and stopped the buzzer of the alarm.
Opening her eyes, she looked for Jack, then remembered. Slowly she swung her long legs out of bed and
sat on the edge, trying to forget the previous morning
when West had kissed her awake. She glanced at the
window and the sunshine relieved her. While she was
apple-picking she would not have time to be self-
indulgent with misery or worry about West. Twenty
minutes later she was dressed, had breakfasted,
grabbed her lunch beside her keys, and was heading
for the door. The envelope on the step with West's
handwriting stopped her and, shaking, she stooped to
pick it up, her fingers clumsy as she opened it.

> Dear Amy
>   Instead of apple-picking, design gardens!
>   West.

Stapled to a corner of the page was a cheque made out
to her for several thousand dollars. Eyes wide, she
read it again and noted the money was from West's
personal account, not his business one, and her
shoulders drooped. He was not hiring her as a professional member of his staff, he was helping a friend.
The money would enable her to be independent, keep
her while she visited architects and garden establish-
ments and clubs to demonstrate her ideas and skill,
and later, when she was successful, she could repay
West. Her independence swayed with temptation, but
was followed by the sting that West was paying her off

because he was sorry for her. The thought of his pity was more distasteful than biting into a luscious apple and finding a codlin caterpillar.

She pulled her notepaper from the buffet and hastily wrote a note, then sealed it and his cheque in another envelope. As she drove down the road she popped the letter into West's personal letter box at the farmhouse, then glanced anxiously at her watch. Instead of being early, she was likely to be late on her first morning. When she reached the large orchard, cars were lined up in a paddock near a long shed and Amy raced into place as the foreman began speaking.

Assigned to a team of locals, Amy was aware that she would have to work hard to earn their respect. By the end of the day her speed and rhythm had improved and, to her delight, the others had accepted her and helped her carry the heavy loads. After a week she received her first pay and, as their team had earned bonus figures, she decided the occupation had its good side—the pay, the sunshine, the outdoor activity and the company. Some were travellers who earned their way doing seasonal work, many were neighbouring smallholders and there were students who relied on the harvests for income. Amy received several invitations to visit when she was passing, and twice went with her group to the local hotel but, conscious of the bulbs and the orders at the cottage, she excused herself after a drink. Each evening she returned to the cottage feeling rather like a bruised apple herself, but after a reviving bath or shower and a meal she worked, despite fatigue, to fulfil the daffodil lists.

Although she made an effort, Amy was conscious of an aloneness in her life. She missed Jack O'Day but admitted that not seeing West caused pain. Without West visiting, their occasional meals, their long walks and discussions, life seemed without its sparkle. Sometimes, before she went to bed, her hands would wander over the letters he had written, but she remembered his eyes and grey, taut face when she had said she loved him, and put the letters away.

Rain woke her the next morning and she lay in bed, grateful for the change from the apple-harvesting. During the day she packed the rest of the bulb orders, checked them all and contacted the couriers to check prices. Finding out she could save a little if she dropped the boxes at their offices, she drove into the city, and paid the costs. Pleased that she had fulfilled her aunt's instructions, she handed the neatly tabulated dockets into the solicitor's office. As she returned to the street, a joyous bark greeted her as Jack O'Day rushed up.

'Jack! What are you doing here? You shouldn't be running round dragging your lead! It's good to see you, my lumpy, bumpy puppy.' Patting him, she checked the cars parked along the street but could not see West's familiar wagon. The puzzle was solved when she realised that two doors down was a plant and florist's shop with West Thornton's logo. Her heart pumping as fast as if she had just completed a half-hour run, she picked up Jack's lead and walked into the shop, releasing him as he tugged her towards the staffwork area. A quick inspection told her West was out of sight but she could hear his distinctive, deep voice.

'I was rung up at one o'clock this morning. It seemed a century before she had the baby. A girl! Kerryanne thinks she's beautiful but she's allowed to be biased. Now, I've already sent a pram to the house. What I want you to do is to go there tomorrow, before four, when Arnold brings Kerryanne and the baby home,

and decorate the porch with pot plants and pink
flowers. I'll take this miniature arrangement in a pram
with me.'

Realising she was eavesdropping, Amy slipped out
of the door and back on to the street, but a frown was
on her face. Why had West been rung at one in the
morning to inform him that Kerryanne was going to
hospital to have the baby? Such musings were the
thoughts of a jealous old besom, Amy decided as she
marched back to the car and drove to the supermarket.
When she reached home she would go through the
wool pile and knit a small present for the baby. She
was pleased with the bonus money in her pocket but,
conscious that a few days of wet weather could blow
her planned budget, she bought with frugal care and
left, tall with virtue. Rain reduced her mood as she
drove home; the sun had given up on the day in
disgust.

Lurching up the twin rivulets which marked the
driveway, she wished she could afford loads of gravel.
She steered round the muddy water-filled potholes,
but dodging one she felt a rear wheel sag into another.
Instantly easing, she reversed back and tried again. At
the top of the drive, she released a gusty breath of
concentrated tension, and garaged the car.

Another day of rain enabled her to do some house-
work before packing up extra boxes of bulbs, but she
was pleased the wind blew the rain away in the mid-
afternoon and the next morning was fine. Apple-
picking was hard, but she needed the money!

A birthday celebration of one of her co-pickers kept
her later than usual after work, and when she arrived
at the cottage's open gateway, she stared in surprise.
Gravel had been spread in thick, abundant measure
on her driveway. Nosing the car gingerly up the

shingle, she guessed West was responsible. Instead of being grateful she was irritated; it would have given satisfaction to have marched over to West's office, demanded the cost and been able to write out a cheque. The reality was that she could not afford the pride-saving gesture. Guilty with her lack of graciousness, Amy made a cup of tea while critical thoughts tossed and scratched each other like gemstones in a tumbler. A tapping on the window from a branch of a dogwood reminded her there were some actions she could take.

'Right, *cornus kousa*, you might have wonderful scarlet leaves, but you've given me more than one fright on the last two windy evenings!' She finished her tea and went to the shed for the secateurs.

It took seconds to snip off the offending branch, plus two more which reached for the pane. They were attractive and she relaxed as she wandered round the garden looking for flowers to arrange with them. She found several yellow-orange chrysanthemums which went well against the dogwood then, remembering her bedroom rose needed replacing, she walked through to the hidden garden. Few red roses still bloomed, but the symbol of love offered one open bloom and she left the two buds which kept their petals tight-wrapped against the chill of twilight.

Inside, she steeped the flowers in the bathroom basin and began running her bath, then went upstairs for a change of clothes. The sound of Jack O'Day's woofling drew her downstairs in time to hear West's knock. Hooking her clothes on the bathroom peg, she hurried to open the door.

'Good evening, West. Thank you for the new gravel on my drive. In time, I'll repay you.' Her words were stiff yet, when she saw regret in West's eyes, she felt small.

'You're angry, Amy. I was trying to help. You wouldn't accept my cheque. I wanted to apologise for my comments the other night. You were right, I was trying to pick a fight with you. If it's any consolation, the shame has been nagging me like toothache since.' His hand went to the creature at his side. 'Jack O'Day has missed you too. Every night when we go out for a walk, he heads over here. I take him to the beach and he ignores the seagulls and walks beside me like a penitent.'

'I've missed you both,' Amy admitted. She hid her emotion by bending to cuddle Jack. 'He likes a walk in my orchard—it took me a while to figure out why. He eats the windfalls! Cupboard love!' She plucked for another neutral line. 'He's grown in a week. Taller and broader?' She risked looking at West and saw weariness in his stance, his neck bent, arms slack. Her heart ached. She wanted to hold and comfort him, make him smile; instead her fingers played with Jack's collar. In the silence she gained courage.

'You're tired, West. Something wrong?'

'You're too observant, Amy. I've been working on a project hybridising for a certain rose, the way your aunt taught me, since I was fourteen and I had hoped this summer I would achieve success, but it didn't happen. This afternoon I finished the notes, and I seem little further ahead. But there's next summer and the summer after that. . .' He thrust his hand through his hair so that for a moment he was a lad again. 'My problem is time. I've done the colour graphs, but there are six hundred seedling results to compare with thousands of previous years. There's basic matching of chromosomes, the sets of sevens. . . I've spent hours at the computer and only established that certain patterns won't work. A glance at the bloom would have given me the same answer!' His smile was reluctant but it lifted his face. 'What about you, Miss Independence Radcliffe? Apple-picking suits you; you look wonderful!'

'In these?' Amy pointed to her work clothes, faded blue jeans and a light red shirt, and laughed.

'You remind me of a ripe apple, full of vitality and sunshine.'

'A very grubby apple. I was just running the bath,' she remembered and raced back, but the water met her halfway. 'Oh no! I left the taps running!' She ran to the bathroom, warm water sloshing over her feet, and dropped the dragons' tails.

West's chuckle was joined by Jack's excited barking.

'Throw down some towels, I'll help you mop it up, Amy.' He was already taking off his shoes and socks and removing his jacket. Working together, they placed the towels, wrung them out into buckets, and repeated the performance many times. Jack, convinced it was a new game, decided to drag a towel too, but was tackled by West. Amy, perched temporarily on the side of the bath, laughed as Jack, with footballer's agility dodged, catching West off-balance. She applauded as West stood up but as he came towards her, she bent back, realising his intent. The next instant she was splashing in the warm bath and it was West's turn to laugh.

'You goofball! All my clothes are wet!' Amy protested with a smile as she wiped her streaming hair from her eyes.

His breath was a warm chuckle as he leaned over her to dry her face with a towel. 'You said you were grubby!'

The laughter between them gave way to silence as they looked at each other. Amy was aware of the intensity of his eyes, the darkening shadow of his beardline and the curve of his lips. Leaning back against his wrist so that his arm was supporting her head from the water, she closed her eyes. She found the gentleness of his kiss a questioning permission, and as she answered generously he kissed her lingeringly. Everything was forgotten except the pleasure of his touch. When he kissed her ear, the thrill caused her to lie back, but her movement sent a wave of water surprising them and they both spluttered into laughter.

'Amy, you smell of apples, I'll start eating you,' he teased as he shook back the water from his hair. 'Ever tried apple-bobbing?'

Smiling, she looked at West and the tenderness on his face made her heart sing. Before she had time to speak they were distracted by the sight of Jack O'Day, possibly imagining himself invisible because he had turned his back, dragging a wet towel Amy had left by the basin of flowers. A branch of the dogwood had snagged in it and the flowers cascaded down.

'Jack! Stop that! Drop it!'

'That rose! Amy, look at the colour!'

More concerned with the progress of the towel, she looked back at West to see the reverent way he picked up the bloom.

'Amy, it's a miracle!' He turned it slowly. 'A beauty! Excellent hybrid tea shape, a strong neck, firm petals well anchored. . .and I can smell its perfume from here! The perfect red rose! Looks as if I lost the race.' He glanced across at her to explain. 'My pet project. Trying to breed a red rose like this.'

'There are dozens of red roses!'

'But not this colour. They are too blue-red or

orange-red. I thought I knew every red in existence! Someone's beaten me to it. The symbol of love.' He kept turning the bloom, studying every petal. 'It glows! Ouch! You've picked this yourself. A grower would have removed those couple of thorns. Where did you get it?'

'The garden.'

'The garden? Here?' he looked at her, his eyebrows marking disbelief, but the other flowers and foliage had convinced him. 'Come on, out of that bath! Quick, show me! Please!'

'Am I allowed to get dry and dressed?' Amy was hurt. West was more interested in the symbol of love than in being loved and giving love. As he closed the bathroom door she sensed his impatience of the delay. She tugged off the wet clothes, washed her body briefly then, standing up, she pulled the plug on her dreams. Taking her time, she dried herself, put on fresh clothes and wrapped her hair turbanstyle in the last clean dry towel. The floor was damp to her feet as she put the rest of the flowers back into the basin. Taking her wet clothes and the bucket of towels, she dropped them into the laundry tub. In the kitchen, West had placed the red rose in a glass of water and he was seated like a lover, studying it.

'Amy, I can't understand how I haven't seen it! The number of times I've been over here!'

'It's in the hidden rose garden.'

'Of course! Aunt Jean bought a dozen classic reds and grafted cuttings and used a few of my toss-out seedlings. I haven't been there for ages; she shut the gate after the accident, although I offered help.'

Amy leading the way heard West whistle as he saw the tangle of growth hiding the rose garden. 'A friend described gardening as molesting nature,' Amy chuckled, 'but I think she'd change her mind if she saw this section.' She reached the gate. 'I've almost finished weeding in here. Just the last two rows. The one you want must have been among the last planted. It's on the outside, fifth from the end, but there are only a couple more tight buds on the bush.'

'It's not a sport, it's a seedling.' West had stopped beside the rose. 'You beauty! Two blooms just about to open,' he breathed. 'Not a sign of mildew or rust or blackspot! Amy, name your price. I've just got to have this bush and access to it.'

She wanted to say, 'Your love,' but it was not a gift he could give. 'One smile,' she managed. When he looked at her and smiled, she almost lost control. To hide her emotion she looked down and yanked at some weeds by the roots, so revealing a hybridising marker. Wordlessly she picked it up; the thick black numerals were faded but legible. She recognised his style. 'This looks as if it came from you, West.'

'Yes, it's my coding.' West was already taking note of the numbers.

'What's wrong? You're frowning.'

'Part of the sequence is missing. There should be something like T for throwout then MF for malformed or NR for non-recurring. My gardeners look for my letters for the instruction for each plant. This one must have been shifted before I saw it bloom.' He shrugged his shoulders. 'Mistakes do occur. One year I lost five roses off the end of one row. Bless Aunt Jean for keeping it and the marker.'

'She was a hybridist—it would have been anathema to throw out the record.' Amy went to the neighbouring bush and scratched at the base. 'Another of your markers. This one has the numerals then T, B-NP.'

'Blue-red and no perfume.' West pointed to a surviving bloom. 'An official throwout!'

'It's quite pretty——' Amy sniffed '—but I agree with your judgement, because it has no scent. A rose without perfume is like a night without stars.' Reaching into her pocket, she walked past West to snip back the growth from the bush on the other side. A stray branch threatened, and as she clipped it back she read the protruding marker. 'Here's another you haven't seen.' She pointed to the marker, then frowned as a thought took hold. It took her a few minutes to check the last three in the row. There were no letters on the markers, only numbers. 'These are your missing five. You lost them three years ago?'

'Yes.' West managed a twisted smile. 'I've grown thousands of seedlings and the one I wanted was thrown out! This particular sequence was the most promising of my computer results but the seedlings disappointed. Decent reds and some were hardy, but not the perfection I wanted. I didn't bother resowing for the missing few. . . So much time in my own rose field and I never thought to glance in here!' West stood up. 'Amy, the bush is safe here but I'd like to ask you to keep its existence secret. I'll take some cuttings tonight and with your permission erect a temporary shelter.'

'Is that necessary? It's been completely neglected yet it's formed up into a good, strong bush.'

'I don't want to take any risks. It's too valuable, Amy. The strength and form are inherited from its maternal grandmother. If only I'd seen it sooner! Did you notice anything about it?'

'The flowers are a well-shaped, scented hybrid tea,' Amy admitted. 'It had borne a great number of flowers before I arrived. I remember trimming most of the hips off to keep it flowering. When I first saw it, I wondered what it was called. I couldn't remember any rose quite like it, the colour is such a singing red. I've picked a bud for my bedroom regularly and it opens well in the vase.'

'You're describing a champion, Amy! I'll run back for my gear.' He looked around. 'Where's Jack O'Day?'

'Eating windfalls in the orchard.' Amy pointed uphill. 'I'll give him a quick run while you work here.'

'Thanks, my turbanned princess.'

Amy put her hand to the towel round her damp hair but West had sprinted off, engrossed with the rose. Walking back to the cottage, Amy swallowed the lump of hurt in her throat, blaming herself for the unceremonious dumping of her dreams. Hadn't West told her that he did not love her? Why did she keep on hoping? Irritated, she yanked at the towel, pulling it off, combed her hair into place, grabbed her jacket and set off up the hill. She whistled to Jack and he bounced back to her, his enthusiasm cheering. In the orchard there were a number of windfall apples and she made a mental note to find time to make apple jelly. Jack was crunching on one, his enjoyment a recommendation.

'Instead of Jack O'Day, you should be Jack O'Food!' she murmured as she led the way along the terrace. Looking down, she could see the cottage and West among the rose bushes. As though their thoughts had met, he looked up and waved. She saw him pick up a tray of cuttings, carrying it back to the gap in the hedge. When she looked round for Jack he had sneaked back to the orchard for another apple.

'Come on, Jack, it's time to go home, it's cold!' she called as she headed back down. By the time they reached the garden West had set up a temporary mesh fence and was rolling up the additional material. Amy picked up some equipment. 'I'll carry this for you.'

When he smiled his thanks, Amy struggled for nonchalant acceptance. The gate was open between their properties and the security lights flicked on as they approached the main building. West touched an electronic device and the door swung back, to close after their entry.

'Along here, to the lab but first, kennel, Jack.' West paused at a door. Jack pawed a black mark and the door opened. Amy's eyes widened.

'Electronic wizardry! The kennel opens into the courtyard but only Jack's paw opens it. He has a large enclosed area and at the same time we preserve security.'

'All home comforts!'

'A few,' West agreed as he set down the tray and again inserted an access card. 'My lab.'

Amy looked around. An elongated bench-style desk held papers and a computer monitor and keyboard and printer, linked to a high tech microscope. Beyond, she could see the room opened out and there were similar desks and equipment. Trays of seeds and bowls holding sprouting seeds were in spectrum-lit cabinets. 'Impressive!'

'It's an exciting area.'

She held up his equipment and he gestured behind her to a vast-cupboard like area where everything was set out in meticulous order.

'Put them in the first cleaning tray, thanks, Amy.' West had moved to another doorway. 'I'll just wash my hands. Turn left and you'll see the door to the lounge. I'll be with you in a moment.'

The lounge was off a reception area and on the low

coffee table three different roses had been placed in a harmonious line.

West walked to a cupboard concealing a bar and poured out two drinks. 'A celebration!' He handed her a glass. 'Then, dinner. We've a lot to discuss. Do you realise how valuable the red rose will be, Amy? I'd like us to form a separate company to grow and market it——'

'It's your rose! The markers prove it!'

'It was growing in your aunt's garden. Finish your drink. I'm starving.'

'But I'm not dressed. . .'

'A statement I have to deny.' West's dark eyes lit with laughter. 'Come on! One of my friends owns a Chinese restaurant. Cantonese food, the thought of it makes me hungry!'

Amy's heart lifted but then she remembered how West, after kissing her so passionately, had been so easily distracted by the red rose. The man was not in love with her. 'I'll say no to dinner, West.' She felt his searching, dark-eyed gaze.

'Can you tell me why?'

'These past days without you. . .it's been difficult.' She toyed with her drink, revolving the amber fluid in the crystal.

'Amy, can you appreciate what we do have and take it from there? A very special friendship. Let's go out and eat together. It's late, we're hungry and you told me you like Cantonese food. I'll introduce you to my friend, the proprietor, he's a *rosa chinensis* expert.' West's eyes defeated her judgement.

The restaurant was not a pretentious establishment but the red wallpaper and red and gold lanterns gave atmosphere. Red and pink roses overflowing a vase by the cashier's desk made them both smile.

'Red is the colour of the day!' Amy chuckled.

'Red is a colour for happiness in the Orient. You'll have noticed they were old roses. My friend's grandfather remembered them growing near his parents' house in China and I was asked to supply seventy bushes for the old man's seventieth birthday. It was difficult but I managed a good collection. Since then the whole family has become hooked on them——' he gave a lightning smile '—and the proprietor's now quite an authority.'

Moments later, Amy was introduced to the owner who had been informed of their presence by younger members of the family. Greetings exchanged, Amy was given one of the roses plucked from the arrangement.

'*Si Ji Hong*, Four Seasons Red,' Amy named it. 'A magnificent red rose. I love its peony-like shape, thank you.'

'You know roses? Did you know that it was a rose from China which gave the remontant flowering to hybrids?' the proprietor asked her with a glisten of pride.

'Most agree it was *rosa chinensis semperflorens.*' Amy, smiling back, indulged in revealing a little botanical erudition. 'And it led to the development of possibly the first hybrid perpetual, the double red, scented *Rose du Roi* in 1816.' She chuckled at the proprietor's expression of delight. 'My mother is a rosarian in Auckland!'

'Next summer you must bring her to visit our rose garden. For you and West, we will cook some special dishes.'

An array of tantalising and delectable titbits began arriving at their table and Amy appreciated West's comments on some of the delicacies. When the main dishes appeared Amy saw they were being given a banquet. West entertained her with stories of the cuisine, explaining that he had exchanged legends of old roses for some about the food. Their conversation was easy, with frequent laughter, and as she refused the last dish, pleading that her appetite admitted defeat, Amy acknowledged that being with West made her happy. Sipping the mildly astringent pink tea she studied him and saw he was relaxed, the earlier fatigue gone, his dark eyes shining.

'Amy, we haven't mentioned the rose. I think we must discuss it and agree on a partnership. It is valuable.'

'If I had any claim, and that is doubtful. I sold it for a smile, remember!'

'About two thousand and two hundred years ago a Chinese Emperor, Wu Di, walking with his concubine, Li Juan, said, "This rose is just like your smile". And she reminded him, "A smile cannot be bought, surely?" And the emperor was pleased with her wisdom and gave her fifty kilos of gold and everyone smiled!' West's black eyes lit. 'Another story from my friend here, but lawyers prefer a documented base. When we pick up Jack O'Day, I'll write a proposal down and you can get your lawyer to check it. Once the testing's done, I'll begin the registration of Plant Breeders Rights under the Plant Varieties Act to protect our interests.'

'You sound knowledgeable!'

'I've done it before. In my search for the perfect red I developed several lines. One of my earlier seedlings I recrossed to produce a deep red with the reverse of the petals lined with pink. It's a free-flowering flori-bunda, healthy and vigorous. I named it as a tribute to my parents and an agent advised me to register it. It's proving popular, and each time it's sold the company gets a royalty. It turned my hobby into a commercial venture.' He smiled. 'I told you the tax man loves me! I've registered two others, an orange-red and a peony-form pink cluster rose which owes a lot to *Si Ji Hong*. Excuse me a moment. I'll settle the account and then we should go.'

'I'll pay half. It was a superb meal.' Amy reached for her bag.

'You might be independent, Amy, but this was my pleasure. If you want to pay me back, think of a name for our rose.'

Amy stood, pulled her jacket on, picked up her rose and joined him to pass on her compliments. Outside, rain had washed the roads and a brisk wind made Amy shiver. West put his arm around her, comforting and warming. She wanted to enfold herself in his arms and be kissed, but his gesture was protective rather than sexual.

'No apple-picking tomorrow!' She attempted casual-ness, but his touch was making her tremble. With rollercoaster emotions she felt him move away as they reached the vehicle.

The road ribboned black silk and the shadows at the side flared and folded in the headlights. She studied West, knowing his concentration was on the route. In the dark she couldn't see his beautiful Aroha eyes.

'Aroha!' She saw lines draw his eyebrows in at the mention of love. 'Arohanui! For the name of the rose. The Maori word for all-encompassing love. You also honour your ancestor, the plants-woman.'

'Arohanui!' West savoured the name as he turned the wagon into the cottage driveway. 'Sounds good. It's a possibility.'

'I thought we were going back to the office.'

'It was selfish of me, I thought better of it when you were shivering in town. We've had a long day, if fruitful,' he added gently. 'I'll go over and pick up Jack. Paperwork can wait.'

'Of course.' The words were tight in her throat and she turned to open the door to hide the dismay she felt at leaving him. She accepted his escort to the door and his quick check of the cottage without betraying herself.

'Goodnight, Amy.'

Once she heard the departure of the wagon she threw her bag on to the table in frustration. Couldn't he see that loving him and knowing her feelings were not reciprocated was twisting and doubling her pain? Why couldn't he pretend? Why couldn't he love her?

CHAPTER SEVEN

'THANKS, everyone, that's the crop harvested for this orchard.' The foreman's face opened to a chipped-tooth grin. 'Early finish! Today's tallies are being added to your pay so there will be a slight delay. Tomorrow, we start the Gala crop at Kerryanne and Arnold Webster's place. It's on Stone Cottage Road, so new chums ask Amy for directions. It's named for her house.'

Amy acknowledged the foreman's words, but she was glad only a couple needed directions. She wanted to collect her money and take advantage of the chance to get to the bank and pay some accounts. A short time later, money bulging in her wallet, she drove to the cottage, had a hasty shower and put on a green skirt, lacy jersey and green tam o'shanter, enjoying the reprieve from her working clothes. In town she went to the bank, then paid her electricity bill and the instalmant on the wallpaper, and purchased another pair of heavy-duty garden gloves. In a nearby shop a red evening dress on display in the window became a flag of yearning in her vision. She drifted closer, admiring, knowing the colour would suit her skin and hair. She could see herself wearing it, dancing with West; he might even fall in love. . .

'You look like a child outside a chocolate shop!'

'West!' Surprise tugged out the name. His presence filled her with sunshine; it was good just to see him. Recovering her social skills, she gestured to the frock, 'I was just admiring it.'

'Red! And with roses! It's your dress, Amy. Try it on.'

'It's probably not my size,' she muttered. 'Besides, look at the fabric, the way it flows. That's a fine wool crêpe, and the hand-made roses on one shoulder line. . .it's a designer garment. Expensive! Not exactly *de rigueur* for apple-picking!'

'You remind me of one of Aesop's fables. Something about the grapes being sour in any case!' West chuckled. 'I'll buy it for you but there's a catch—you have to allow me to take you to the Country Club ball.'

'It is beautiful.' Temptation and the thought of dancing with West lured with butterfly wings.

'So are you, a perfect combination.'

Amy withdrew her gaze from the gown. 'West, you know I can't accept such a gift.' She made an effort to smile. 'But tell me more about the ball. I love dancing.'

'In three weeks' time. An excuse to dress up and have fun. We'll make up a party with Sue and Jonathon and a few others. Kerryanne is spitting mad because she doesn't think she'll be able to fit into the dress she bought for it months ago!' Laughter lines crinkled his mouth. 'Now, would it be improper for me to buy a friend like Kerryanne a dress?'

'Stop teasing, West! I'm not going to make judgements on a situation which has nothing to do with me.'

'If you're sure you don't want it, would you try on the frock so I could see if it would fit?'

Amy, feelings outraged, looked at West in disbelief. It was her frock! It even had their red roses on it! How could he be so insensitive? Guilt began seeping into her anger. Wasn't there another fable about a dog in a manger? West had offered it to her and she had turned

him down. Hadn't she so righteously informed him
that she wasn't going to make judgements?

Back stiff, shoulders indignant, Amy walked into
the shop, asked the size of the red rose dress and
allowed herself to be shown to the cubicle area to
change and comb out her hair while the attendant
undid the mannequin. When the gown was carried in
Amy sighed, appreciating its warm colour and skilled
workmanship close up. In a renegade moment she
almost told the attendant to remove it, but she slipped
it on, unable to resist. Moulding to her body, the fit
was perfect and as she looked in the mirror the graceful
lines reflected melted her anger. Adjusting her bra
straps she smoothed the garment into place. She had
never worn anything which suited her so well. Preen-
ing, she decided that she looked beautiful, and the
knowledge stunned. For so long she had been a gawky
giraffe, but the gown revealed an elegant, tall, young
woman. West was a man who appreciated beauty.

There was no price ticket and she guessed West had
commandeered it before she could see it; but she knew
even if she used the savings for the rate money, she
wouldn't have enough. She was tempted to tell West
she'd changed her mind, but shrapnel of conscience bit
and she forced herself to remember that she had put
the gown on so that he could have some idea of the fit
for Kerryanne. She frowned. Kerryanne was at least
five inches shorter and her body shape rounded. Why
should West buy such a gift for his former lover? But
why not? He was an old friend and a generous one.
Would Arnold be hurt? Slamming the thoughts away,
she viewed herself critically and reached in her purse
for make-up, deepening the shading round her eyes
and adding more lipstick, noting it was the exact
match. The ruby earrings would be perfect.

For a few minutes the red dress was hers and she would enjoy wearing it. She could pretend West was picking her up for the ball. Soon they would be dancing, the red dress showing off her figure as she moved. . . The musak which had been softly annoying changed to a waltz melody. Opening the curtain she stood still enjoying West's pleasure. With sensual deliberation she walked in time to the music towards him.

'You're beautiful, Amy.'

The sincerity in his low voice and the look in his dark eyes rewarded her.

'Our dance, I think,' he murmured, leading her towards a tiled area by the counter.

It seemed natural to dance, and when the music changed again and broke the mood, Amy accepted the assistants' applause with a curtsy. The fantasy was over and she could not look at West, could not bring herself to ask if the dress would suit Kerryanne. The thought of it being worn by a woman with whom West had shared part of his life was bitter aloes. Admitting silently that there was a definite improvement needed in her character, Amy returned to the cubicle and with care removed the dress. She did not want to give it to the assistant, she wanted to say she would put a deposit on the dress and pay it off. If she could borrow from her parents. . . If she took a ticket in the weekly lottery, she might win. . . Reality forced her to hand it to the assistant. In the mirror, Amy saw the wetness of tears in her eyes and she blew her nose and reapplied some powder before slipping on her skirt and jersey. Yanking her tam o'shanter on at a brave angle, she stepped out.

West was talking to the sales staff and Amy noted their attentive smiles. Her emotions see-sawed—the red dress was tissue-wrapped and as she watched it was handed to West.

'Coffee?' West questioned as he led the way to the street. 'I want to go through some papers regarding our rose partnership and I've twenty minutes before my next appointment.' He paused beside her car. 'Why don't you put this parcel inside? Saves lugging it around.'

It was too much! Amy's temper exploded. 'You, you. . .have the sensitivity of a. . .a dead tree stump! Couldn't you see how much I wanted that gown? Yet you asked me to try it on! And it's beautiful. I've never wanted anything so much.' She swiped at a traitorous tear. 'Next you'll be asking me to deliver it to Kerryanne!'

'It's not Kerryanne's name on the label, it's addressed to my red rose partner,' West pointed out, his expression tender. 'I had to trick you, it was the only way I could find out if it fitted, and if you really liked it.'

Amy sniffed noisily.

'Knowing your principles, I had to let the dress undermine your decision,' West grinned as he took her car keys from her hand, unlocked the door, dropped the parcel safely out of sight and relocked the car. 'But I loved watching your face with conscience and temptation doing battle! Especially as you'd been so righteous!' His eyes gleamed with laughter as he lifted a wayward curl from her face. 'You turned the tables on me, looking sexy and beautiful—only you could wear it so wonderfully. Rose Red! I want you to wear it at the ball and I'm going to be your partner, Ms Radcliffe.'

'I don't know what to say,' Amy murmured.

'The obvious: thank you!' West guided her across the street and into the coffee-bar. 'Coffee?'

'Thank you.' She saw West's smile. 'I can't refuse the frock, it's just so exquisite. I've never worn something so lovely.'

'Everything about you is beautiful.'

The timbre of his voice, sensual with depth, made her widen her eyes. She warmed under his gaze, his intensity lingering on her overful lower lip. The rattle of the cups was a disturbance. Amy made an effort. 'I'll pay for the coffee.'

'Prove you're still your own woman? Anyone who doubts doesn't know you! This is on the tax man. We have to have somewhere to discuss these papers.'

As soon as they were settled at a private table, West handed over the documents. Amy scanned the first page, noting West had management control for the development and nursery area of the rose, and went on to scan the partnership clause. With surprise, she reread it. 'There's a mistake here. You made it eighty per cent for me, twenty for you. That isn't right. Your typist put it the wrong way round.'

'No, Amy, the figures are correct.'

'Well, you'll not get me to sign this, West. You bred it and we proved it. Reverse the figures and I'll agree. Aunt Jean might have grown it, but. . .' Amy hesitated at the niggling thought but knew it had to be spoken. 'Accidentally, she could have been responsible for removing the five in the first place.'

'No. I checked my records, I employed a man who was swift in his work but careless, he was the culprit. He was fired soon afterwards.' West drank his coffee and slowly lowered his cup. 'You could set up this project on your own, you have the rose, the ground, the knowledge and the horticultural skill but, I believe

I have some right, the necessary capital and the market understanding.'

'Fifty-fifty, West?'

'An equal partnership? Amy, have you looked at the next page, with the map? There's a clause stipulating you supply five hectares as shown. It's the field by the hedge and the first daffodil paddock, some of your best land. You'll be paid market rates for the lease from the partnership once we use it for the rose, but in the meantime, it will be used by my company and you'll be paid from the nursery reserve. It's a fifteen-year lease. I want you to discuss the proposition with your solicitor.'

'I'll have to consult Jonathon and Sue. They've been using most of it for a number of years.'

'At a peppercorn, or rather a side of hogget, rental. I can buy land for Jonathon and Sue in the next valley for a fraction of the price of what your land is worth to me. We talked it over before I made my purchase offer.'

Amy nodded. 'I need some time to think this through, West. I was intending to use some myself.'

'For flowers? We should co-operate. You have the land, you haven't the funds to develop it, but leasing me some will help your cash problem. In spring you'll be busy with the bulbs but you should consider other seasons to give you more spread of income. Cottage-style chrysanthemums grow well outside so you wouldn't need shade houses; they're an excellent cut flower, we have the packing facilities and the market demand is there.'

'Sounds fine.'

'You're being polite! Look, I won't push you into anything but let me help. I know the best people to deal with and the prices. I would appreciate a decision on the five hectares within the next three days; an order depends on it. As it concerns one of the daffodil paddocks I'll arrange for my staff to dig them out for you, and transplant where you wish. Fortunately it's the right time of year.'

'That's a huge task!' Amy's hazel eyes widened at the possibility of the woodland area carpeted with gold. 'I'll call in to see Sue and Jonathon.' Amy pushed the papers back into the envelope. 'I'll take this along to the solicitor, if you insist.'

'It is necessary, Amy. There's a potentially large sum of money involved.'

'Really? Enough for me to have the cottage floors stripped, sanded and limed?'

'Enough to buy a dozen cottages!'

'West! Truly?' Dreams of altering the cottage, redesigning and developing the garden, widened her eyes. West's chuckle brought her back to the hard chair.

'Don't get excited, we've a long period ahead. Years! I'm reluctant to raise your hopes. Just how much money depends on the rose. I wish we had been able to study it from its first flowering. A good point in its favour is the healthy growth. We will have to do further tests. . .'

He ticked off the points on his fingers and Amy found herself studying his hands. An outdoor man's hands, strong, muscular, yet the fingers were long and smooth, proof of the time spent accounting and in his laboratory, where deftness was an essential skill. She remembered the feel of his hands on her skin and wanted to reach out to touch him. How could he make her feel so sexy when he was simply explaining about the rose? She struggled to concentrate.

'. . .the floriferous percentages in different conditions. I think we have a winner, but before we get there we have to submit it for trials around the world. Reds are notoriously fickle. In some climates colour fades; others can't take the cold. Don't forget, Amy, we've only the one bush and an accident could kill it overnight. I'm always wary until I've nursed through more plants. Not every cutting reacts well to the glasshouse, building up stocks is time-consuming, and there are wages of staff and costs of equipment to deduct. But if all goes well——' he smiled '—you'll be able to buy as many red dresses as you can wear!'

'And you didn't accept one smile!' Amy shook her head. 'You're an honourable man, Westleigh Thornton!'

'I've made my share of mistakes!' His eyes revealed self-mockery. 'The rose doesn't solve your immediate problem for cash unless you allow me to give you an advance.'

'It's tempting, but if something goes wrong with the rose I end up in debt to you.'

'You're too proud for your own good! I could advance you the lease on the land for five years. It won't be a fortune but it could help you in the interim.' He pushed away his cup. 'I don't like to see you having such a struggle.'

At the evidence that West cared, she felt the spring of hope gush into a fountain. 'I'm fairly fit and it's only until I get established. Apple-picking does have its. . . no, I won't say lighter side,' she laughed, 'but I've met some interesting people through it. We're working at Kerryanne's and Arnold's place tomorrow.'

'Close to home! You'll have to give my baby a cuddle.' West grinned. 'She's so incredibly tiny!'

'Babies *are* small!' she chuckled, and switched back to her subject. 'With the extra time, I'm hoping to dig and pack some more bulbs. Would you be interested in selling them?'

'Most of the nurseries would have their own suppliers but we could try a special promotion. Perhaps some varieties, in lots of ten, but the price is critical. Ask Sue to arrange an appointment with my nursery manager.' He flicked a glance at his watch. 'Time to go. I'll walk with you to the solicitor's.'

When they parted company Amy went upstairs to the offices and, not expecting an immediate appointment, she left the documents for the lawyer to check and returned to her shopping. She needed the time to consider West's offer. No doubt she would be wise to grow a well-known flower such as the chrysanthemum, but what of her own idea of redesigning the cottage garden, developing a nursery where she could sell a variety of perennials, both flowers and herbs? Would the scheme work? Would it bring in enough to live on? In one area she could set up a no-dig garden, in another use raised beds, the whole garden on organic principle using companion planting. But to lease West the five hectares to one side of the drive would ruin the plan, rows of plants in front of one half of the cottage would make her landscaping looking unbalanced. Could she take some land from both sides to satisfy West and yet still protect her front sweep?

Reaching the car, she drove back to the cottage and it was with glowing pleasure that she hung the red dress in her wardrobe. It was almost dark outside, but she took her large tape, clipboard and some stakes; if she had to measure and counter-offer she had little time. She worked until sightlines were invisible and rose at dawn to continue until she was due at the Websters'.

The first day she didn't see Kerryanne or the baby

and she remembered the gift she had started—time seemed to be running away with her. After work she walked along to see Sue and Jonathon, was invited to have tea *en famille*, and Sue made an appointment with the nursery manager for five o'clock the next day. At exactly five Amy was at the receptionist's desk and was ushered into the office of the nursery manager. He was a pleasant man with an enormous respect for her aunt's work and Amy warmed to him. They discussed a range of possibilities for the daffodils, and when she left Amy had a definite order at an excellent price. Leaping for joy, she ran through the daffodil fields back to the cottage.

'I'll be able to redecorate the kitchen, maybe more!' Amy said to Jack O'Day who had followed her. 'Maybe I could even think about having a dog, just like you!' She skipped into the kitchen, picked up the phone and dialled. 'Sue? Amy. Just rang to thank you for setting up the meeting with the manager. It's made everything so much easier. I can stand straight and look the mailbox in the eye!'

'That's grand. Did you know there's a local ball soon? I wonder if I could hint to West to invite you. . . He's asked you already? I must tell Jonathon! That's great news. You and West are so suited, two peas in a pod! I hope it works out for you.'

The words echoed as she replaced the receiver, regret and yearning filling Amy's mind as she went to bed. She was restless during the night, her dreams broken several times by vivid images of being kissed by West. In the morning Amy was about to eat breakfast when the solicitor rang, suggesting a late afternoon appointment. She explained her proposed changes and the reasons and agreed to the meeting. There was no time for breakfast or packing a lunch, and as their team figures had fallen they cut their lunch break to make up the figures. It was a rush to change and drive to town and on the way Amy knew she should have taken five minutes to have made a sandwich. A headache niggled a warning. Trying to ignore it, she discussed the land details and attached the map, the solicitor informing her that Dr Thornton would have to approve the split of the five hectares and the change in the time plan of the lease. Confident that West would agree, she signed the papers and then the solicitor moved on to discuss the final documents for her aunt's estate. The summaries blurred before her eyes, her head was a parade ground for a dozen drummers practising for a tattoo, and the reminders of her aunt were all too much. Excusing herself she left, and almost fainted going down the stairs.

With relief she saw the sign for the Chinese restaurant. The proprietor led her to a chair and returned a moment later with a bowl of soup and bread. Amy ate shakily, her headache less thunderous as the food nourished.

'Now, Miss Radcliffe, relax; you look the colour of my husband's white rose!' The proprietor's wife joined her. 'I'll cook some chicken breast and rice for you, delicate and tasty.'

'I'm better already. I should have eaten earlier,' Amy admitted. 'But I'd love some of your chicken and rice. I'm very hungry!'

Amy recovered quickly as she ate and was able to enjoy being fussed over. A faint thrumming echoed where the headache had been, so she drove home slowly and went straight to bed. The next day she had a good breakfast before she went out, and made sure she packed an adequate lunch. She had finished it and returned to her perch when she saw Kerryanne, with

Arnold tenderly carrying the baby, walk down from the house. The sight was warming and, with most of the other pickers, she ran down the path to greet them.

A tiny, alert face surrounded by a scalp of fine dark hair peeped from the folds of a shawl, as though she wanted to observe everything that was happening. Beautiful dark eyes seemed to focus on Amy. She was glad Kerryanne and Arnold were surrounded by admirers; her stunned reaction would have been impossible to hide in a one-to-one situation. The baby was the image of West!

The *döppelgänger* knowledge burnt as she worked. She had thought West so honourable! Such a good man! Believed him when he explained his former relationship with Kerryanne. Yet there had been pointers—the intimacy between West and Kerryanne, the conversation she had heard at his shop, the fact that West had been informed before Kerryanne was taken to the hospital; when she announced she was to work at the Websters' orchard, West had told her to 'give my baby a cuddle'. Had he been trying to prepare her? Was West acknowledged as the father between Arnold and Kerryanne? Yet the pair seemed so happy, so united, a natural couple. Arnold looked an easy-going man, but in his conversation at the packing room he had several times been firm. He would be devastated if he thought his wife had been unfaithful. But the evidence was there in the baby's eyes. The baby didn't fit with his two red-haired brothers, who took after their sandy-haired father. Could there be another explanation?

She emptied a load of apples and returned to the row, mind preoccupied. Had West been visiting her at Stone Cottage as a way of distracting attention from his renewed affair with Kerryanne? He was a deeply sensual man, but she had thought him responsible. He had teased her about having children, like so many chickens. Her Papageno! They had even discussed the genetic chances of having a dark-eyed baby! With him as the father, he had said it would be inevitable, the Aroha family gene was a dominant one. He had wanted to settle down, have the comfort of a supportive wife and children. . .but he did not want love.

Was it because he had never stopped loving Kerryanne? Was the story of Melissa just a fantasy? The claim of recent celibacy another string to protect Arnold's wife?

Possibilities chased each other like children playing hide-and-seek. When the afternoon's work was finished she trudged up the hill to her house in near despair. Unable to cope with clamouring thoughts, she viewed the daffodil field and decided to start the long process of digging and lifting the bulbs for sale. Dark stopped her efforts and she gathered her bulbs and tools and put them away. The physical effort and the concentration necessary to separate and code the bulbs had kept her mind from focusing on West for an hour.

The questions returned to haunt her in the bath. She could picture him standing against the doorway, his magical eyes gleaming, his mouth curved in appreciation. He was a dominating, virile man, his physical strength honed by years of farm work, and he was also a scholar and businessman, thoughtful and responsible. Responsible! The word kept returning to mock. Unless she had seen the baby's likeness for herself, she would not have believed West's irresponsibility.

Somehow she forced herself to cook and eat a meal and prepare her clothes for the next morning. She moved like an automaton, going upstairs to bed emotionally exhausted. As she lay in her narrow cot, memories crowded her; West advancing on her angrily when he thought she was pinching the bulbs, apologising with a hundred creamy roses, whistling as she crossed the roadway, writing to her when he was overseas, his passionate return and his reaction when she told him she loved him. There had been agony in his regret.

To West, love was important. '. . .you give me your hopes, your dreams, your life, and I have nothing to give you'. Instead of taking advantage of her emotions and making love to her, he had walked away, tried to stay away, because he believed it was best for her. Such a man would not have fathered Kerryanne's child. She sat up in bed convinced she was right. The man she loved was a good man. Hadn't he offered her the partnership of the rose when he needn't have involved her at all? Wasn't that proof of his integrity? Or was it, too, part of the cover up? Did she trust West? Was it possible to not trust a man and yet love him?

CHAPTER EIGHT

AMY reached for the pink-wrapped and beribboned packet from her day pack and walked towards the Webster farmhouse. Apart from the first visit to the orchard there had been only glimpses of Kerryanne during the harvest days, so Amy had convinced herself that she had imagined the baby's likeness to West. The gravel crunched under her feet and she saw Kerryanne look up from her meal preparations at an outdoor table and wave to her.

'A small present for the baby.'

'Amy, how charming; the package looks so pretty it's almost a shame to open it!' She bent to one side and swung the glistening parcel. 'For you, little one, but I'll undo the ribbons!'

The baby was lying on the rug looking up at her. Amy's heart missed a beat as two deep brown eyes gazed back. West's eyes! The baby reached out long fingers towards the ribbons and, dimly, Amy heard Kerryanne admiring the rainbow doll she had knitted.

'It's wonderful, such bright, happy colours, Amy. Look, the baby likes it! Have you time for a drink? You must be ready for one after picking apples all day. Arnold and I usually have one now.'

Kerryanne's offer penetrated Amy's thoughts. She scrambled to escape. 'I'm rushing to get some bulbs dug and packed up. With the shortening twilights I only have an hour.'

'In the winter we'll have a chance to get to know you better. This is such a hectic time. It's a good year for us, Arnold says the best ever. Our little Aroha has brought us luck!'

'Aroha?'

'The baby. West suggested it. A family name and she is a baby of love.'

Amy blurted words. 'She is beautiful. Such magnificent eyes!'

'From her father. And her long fingers. I think I may have contributed my dimples!' Kerryanne put the doll beside the rug and the baby examined it. 'Amy, I wanted to talk to you. West told me he explained our relationship. You must be aware of how close we three are and how much that depth of friendship means to us. West assured me you were mature enough to understand, but jealousy is destructive. You must know I love my husband.'

A chirpy whistle announced Arnold's approach and stopped Amy from questioning Kerryanne.

'Amy, we'll be finished harvesting tomorrow and someone said you're taking a break. Come over one day and we can have a natter——' Kerryanne looked from Amy to her husband '—women's talk, sweet man of mine. Amy's going to the ball with West!' She turned back to Amy. 'You'll have to learn to share West, he's an excellent dancer. . . My Arnold steps as if he's wearing gumboots.' She slipped her arm around her husband to soften the criticism.

Amy picked up her backpack, managed to say farewell and walked out of the gate. By the time she had reached her cottage, she was sick. The baby did not resemble Arnold or Kerryanne. Many babies had dark hair, but the steady gaze, the intelligence of expression were West's. Kerryanne's open admission that the baby's eyes and hands were from her father made Amy shiver. West's strong, long-fingered hands had held her, touched her. Arnold had grey-blue eyes. She had noticed them as he smiled so lovingly at his wife. Had Kerryanne been telling her that West was the father? What had the comments about the depth of friendship meant? The baby of love? Kerryanne claimed to love Arnold. Could Arnold not father children? Had West donated sperm? The thought was dismissed when she remembered the older children.

Were West and Kerryanne conducting a long-term affair? If so it would make nonsense of everything West had told her. Could that be why Kerryanne had said she would have to learn to share West? Nausea gripped Amy and she paused, catching her breath before climbing the last few paces towards the cottage. West had been informed when Kerryanne went into labour and he had been among the first to see the baby. He had given the baby her name. Aroha, 'perfect love', the name she had suggested for the red rose, Amy thought with bitterness. Also the name of West's great-great-grandmother and her daughter, earthwomen, the ancestors whose genes had given West his striking dark eyes and his flair with plants. Kerryanne had admitted to its being a name from West's family. The floral welcome for the baby and his instruction 'Give my baby a cuddle' assumed more significance. It was his baby. He had told so many glib lies.

Shivering, stomach churning, Amy ran for the toilet, and tried to stem her misery by staring at the porcelain. The heavy, old-fashioned roses that formed a bowl garland failed to impinge on her consciousness.

Cold, flesh in purple and orange goosebumps, she stood up, the nausea past. Numbed with misery, she could not relax. Instead she moved out to the garden shed and collected some boxes and the forks. There was satisfaction in forcing the ground apart, using the anger which erupted into a savage emotion. She wanted to hurt West, hit, strike, flail him.

Tears fell on to the handle of the fork and plopped into the holes as she lifted the bulbs. She wiped back the tears. In her rage she worked quickly, but after an hour night forced her to stop as she could not read the tag numbers beside each patch of bulbs. Collecting the line of bulbs and boxes, Amy paused—she had intended to sell them through West's nursery. How could she deal with a man who lied?

Habit helped her clean her implements and put them away, but she left the bulbs on the bench. Aching in every part of her body, she ran a hot bath, adding fragrant oil to soothe. The aroma helped her relax until memory taunted her that she had signed a legal agreement to be partners with West with the rose. She jumped out, hastily dried, threw on her towelling gown and ran to the telephone. The legal offices would be closed but she knew her solicitor frequently worked late. As the number began ringing she planned her instructions. With luck, the document would not have been forwarded to West's solicitors; she could withdraw from the contract before West signed, then there would be no legal document binding them. It would deny West access to her five hectares, and as far as she was concerned West could dig up the red rose, and chop the symbol of love for kindling!

The ringing switched to an answerphone. She summarised her instructions and was just finishing when a familiar knock set her heart hammering. Replacing the phone, she struggled to quieten her volatile emotions as she opened the door.

'I missed seeing you in the bath, Amy.' West surveyed her and smiled. 'But greeting me, perfumed and, I think, smoothly naked underneath your wrap is sweet seduction!'

She had forgotten just how attractive he was, the power of his presence and the richness of *crème brulée* in his voice. He reached out to her, but Amy stepped back and pulled the garment tightly into place.

'Did you wish to see me?' Her attempt at formality backfired as the laughter danced in his eyes. Eyes he had passed on to his daughter! 'Blast you, West!'

'Amy!' West's mobile face had formed a frown, wrinkling the twin lines on his forehead and puckering his sculptured lips. 'What's wrong, sweetheart?'

Sweetheart! He had never called her such a tender name before. It sounded so devoted, as if he really did care. . . 'I am not your sweetheart!' Amy lashed. 'How dare you ask me what is wrong? Why couldn't you have told me the truth?'

'I have!'

'Part of the truth! I thought you were a man of honour!' Rage scorned. 'Like being Kerryanne's lover!'

'Ancient history.'

'You're still doing it! Lying by implication!' Anger cracked the dam of her feelings. 'You and Kerryanne were lovers nine months ago! She has your baby!'

West stood tall, his eyes black sparks 'What? Aroha? *Mine*! I told you my sexual relationship with Kerryanne was over years ago. Who told you such lies?'

Each word was sharpened, a stick jabbing her.

'No one! The baby is the image of you!'

'You judge me on that basis? That's ridiculous! You? With your understanding of genetics?' The volcano of rage threatened into a lava spill. 'You love me? You don't know me at all!'

'Love doesn't deny truth!' Amy screamed the words,

saw West stride from the room, the kitchen light elongating his shadow until the night hid him. Tremors raced up and down her body and she became aware of the chill southerly wind and ran to shut and lock the door, making a fortress of the cottage, but she was the prisoner in pain.

Drained of emotion and energy she sat down in the flattened cushions of the old pinewood chair. The look in West's eyes had shrivelled her; she felt old, crabbed. If only she could have remained calm, dignified! Why hadn't she been able to tell West her fears, to ask him for an explanation? Why had she lost her temper? Was it because when she had seen him standing at the door, his smile cosseting, delighting in her appearance, she had ached to be held, caressed and kissed? How could she still want him? Why did he have so much attraction?

They had been two cymbals clashing at each other. West furious with her. Expecting her to accept everything he said! Love didn't ignore logic. With a tightening of her lips, Amy knew she had trusted him until the baby forced her to see another viewpoint. Yet he had been so. . .so outraged!

'You judge me on that basis? That's ridiculous! You? With your understanding of genetics?' His words played like a tape on a loop. What did he mean? Genetic structures and relationships: the effect of one dominant gene could reappear, as Aroha's dark eyes appeared through five generations, as strong as ever. Marty, West's nephew, had the same gift, yet his father had mid-brown eyes and auburn hair. Jonathon could have fathered the baby. The thought bounced off her, Jonathon was like Arnold, steady, loyal, and with a commitment and love of his family.

'You don't know me at all!' West's voice taunted

her. They had discussed parenthood. Hadn't West refused Kerryanne's desire for a child earlier because he had known their future relationship was uncertain? He had given up Melissa, the girl whom he had said he loved, when he discovered she had a husband and two children. In West's book, children were sacred. They had joked about having children together, he had teased her with the Papagena song; Amy squeezed her eyes tight as though to block out the mental movie.

Unhappy and uncertain, she boiled the kettle to make a drink. Steam formed impatient clouds, one bumping into the other against the window, before she switched off the kettle. Knowing she had to eat, she made up a packet of instant soup and ate a chunk of focaccia bread. She had bought two loaves from one of her workmates who passed the bakery, intending to share the treat with West. Breaking another piece from it, she ate knowing that, until she apologised, they would not be companions again. Thinking of her workmates, she realised *they* had not remarked on the baby's likeness to West. Several knew that West visited her regularly and their ribald suggestions about the richest, sexiest man in the district she had laughed off, but no one had said anything about West to her since they had started picking at Webster's. Was the community already knitting together the web of secrets to protect its own?

After a night almost sleepless with the pricks from needles of torment, she walked with stiff legs and back down the road to the Websters' orchard, wishing she could avoid the confrontation but aware that Kerryanne was the key to the truth. On arrival she saw Kerryanne driving out and, emotions exhausted, Amy joined the pickers and began to work, routine helping her. It was the final day of the Websters' crop and the fact comforted. The foreman knew she would be absent for two weeks; she needed the time to dig and pack the daffodils, pick her own apple crop and work on the garden. During the day she watched for Kerryanne's return but it was after four before she heard the car, and the opportunity to talk with Kerryanne alone had to wait. The pressure was on to complete the last row before nightfall.

It was dusk when they finished and Kerryanne and Arnold had brought beer and wine and a barbecue to the packing shed area to celebrate. The children wheeling the baby around in a fine pram, Kerryanne a rotund madonna, Arnold's laughing face lit by cooking flames as he manipulated the long-handled tongs at the barbecue, the sizzle of sausages, chops and fish, the relaxed and tired workers in colourful, grubby outfits, reminded Amy of a medieval picture painted with anachronisms to puzzle the viewer.

With rare cynicism Amy observed Arnold and his wife, but their devoted family act she could not fault. While the tally clerk checked and double-checked the figures, Amy kept in the background, feeling she could not accept the offered food or drink, relieved that others kept their hosts busy. She debated if she should walk home, but the thought of a special trip to collect her wages the next day deterred her. By the time her pay was ready the sky was dark, and she wished she had a torch in her pack as she started down the long, darkened farm track to the road. A couple from her group drove past, then stopped and offered her a lift up the hill.

Usually when she approached the cottage she felt cheered, but as she said goodbye at the door she was dejected. Even the air seemed fouled as though her fight with West had destroyed its freshness and clarity.

Burying her nose in the scent of the new bread her co-worker had brought from town, she hurried inside.

Controlling her imagination, she locked the door and found relief in the familiar room. She ran her bath, poured in a sachet of perfumed oil, selected *Lucia di Lammermoor* and tried to relax. *Lucia* was hardly a sane choice but Amy wallowed in the musical misery. When the disc finished the silence was too powerful, making her edgy, and she put on the radio to have the announcer's company. Knowing it was sensible, she prepared, cooked but only picked at a meal. The lack of sounds disturbed her, but as she prepared for bed she told herself it was always quiet in the country.

Amy woke, aware something was wrong. Usually the grasses rustled, there were small scurryings, birdsong. Instead there was silence. She opened her eyes and pulled a rueful face. From the sunshine burning the curtains she had overslept. She wondered what West was doing, then checked her thoughts. Ahead was a busy day; she had to ring the solicitor, dig more bulbs and try to find a market. Washed and dressed, she opened the top window, wrinkling her nose in distaste. A foetid smell was on the air and she slammed the window back into position. She had smelt something similar before, in the chemical division of nurseries overseas.

Could West have been using some sprays which had drifted over to her property? She ran to the large window which had been jammed shut years before and pulled back the curtains. The paddock next to the hedge and the bulb field on the side of the drive where she had been digging looked strange, the grass lying flat.

Herbicide! The bulbs!

Jumping the stairs two at a time she ran down and checked the back garden. Everything appeared normal and she raced to the front. A metre away from the fence line and along one side of the driveway everything was untouched. But on the other side, the stain of death had burnt everything. The smell in the air was faint but distinctive, reminding her of protective gear. She ran back to the shed and reached for her gumboots, gloves and fork. Somewhere there was a mask, she had seen it. . .her hands clamped on to the packet and she ripped it open. Adjusting the mask, she ran out to the drive and began digging beside it. The grasses and clover on the surface were already juicing, the roots meshed in the poisoned soil withering. A spider had huddled into a black dot but been unable to escape and the sight hurt. Carefully she placed the minuscule body aside. The daffodils? Had they survived? If so, where could she get help to dig them out? West? When he had to be the man responsible?

The telltale spread of the spray showed on the earth. It had seeped deeply, following the vee of the brown summer leaves into the throat of the bulbs. Her immediate hope of rescuing the daffodils was crushed. She walked to another part of the field and dug again, but the same pattern was repeated. With little hope she tried in three more spots, but the spray had been applied meticulously. Nothing had escaped. The herbicide must have been sprayed while she had been picking apples the previous day. If they had finished at their usual time, there might have been a chance of salvaging some of the bulbs. Overnight, thousands of daffodils had been ruined, and soon they would be mush!

West! Dropping the tools she ran across the browning grass, ripping back her mask as she reached the hedge. A couple of flower pickers waved to her, but she didn't notice their greetings, she was too intent on reaching the front office. Inside, the receptionist stopped her.

'I'm sorry, Dr Thornton cannot be disturbed in his laboratory.'

'I'll announce myself!' she called back as she clump-thumped along the corridor. She heard Jack O'Day's welcoming bark but his kennel door had been locked. West wouldn't allow him out if there was danger from spray. Barely pausing in front of the closed laboratory door, she pushed at it and saw West examining something at his microscope. He stood up to meet her.

'I presume you have come to apologise. It might have been more courteous to wait in my office. I am not used to people barging in here.'

'No, I have not come to apologise!' Amy fired back. 'And I'm not used to poison being sprayed on to my property! Why, West?'

'A necessary preparation. The five hectares will be sterilised. We'll control everything that goes into the ground. I don't take any risks with the investment.'

'You didn't need to touch the paddocks. The soil there was excellent loam, it's been built up with natural fertilisers and good husbandry over years! Great-aunt Jean put her precious bulbs in it year after year. Now you've ruined it. You had no right!'

'I don't intend to enter an argument between organic versus chemical controls. My company has a legal right to prepare and nurture the five hectares you leased.' His speech was crisp.

'The five hectares. . . I rang my lawyer to cancel it!'

'I've a copy of the contract. Your solicitor would no doubt have explained that a telephone call is not a way to cancel a written agreement. Whether you like it or not, we are in partnership on this issue. That does not give you the right to come in here. Unless you have something further you wish to say, you will leave!'

Amy felt the colour leave her face at the harsh words. West was granite. She had no doubt that his summary was correct, she should have insisted on organic principles, but he was missing the point of the loss of the bulbs. She looked at him and knew that he would never have ordered their destruction. There had to be a mistake. 'I redrew the area of the five hectares leased in the agreement.'

'I was aware of your changes, but as it was still the contour and soil I required, I agreed. I understood the logic of keeping the cottage garden and bulb fields and drive areas intact; I should have thought of it myself.'

'So why did your staff spray up to the driveway as the original agreement showed?' She was no longer angry; sadness had defeated her. 'You've destroyed half the daffodils.'

'What?'

He seemed genuine, Amy noted. 'Whoever sprayed that poison took it right to the drive.'

'You must be mistaken!'

'Unfortunately, I'm not,' she said with bitterness.

'If what you are saying. . .' He was already tugging on gumboots which stood in a sectioned-off area. 'Are you sure it's not drift?' He led the way from the laboratory.

Amy followed, barely able to keep up, despite the length of her own stride. His examination of the ground was swift.

'I'm sorry, there has been a mistake. My latest instructions were not followed. Naturally, I will compensate you.'

'I don't want money.' She was stung by his offer.

'Dr Thornton, I want all traces of chemical removed, the soil restored to its organic balance, and the bulbs replaced. Now!'

'That's impossible!'

'That's what I want!' She kicked at a clod of sticky earth and a small movement caught her attention. Something had survived! A fat pink worm was heading up to danger. Bending over, she took off her glove, deposited the worm on her palm and carried it across the drive to safety.

'What we want and what we get are two different points. The logical way is to continue the sterilisation process, have the soil dug over, buy bulbs and have them planted. However, it will be difficult to replace the quality of the bulbs.'

'And to rebuild the ecosystems!' Pride helped her march away from him, and she paused only to gather her tools. At the shed she dropped the gloves and the mask in the rubbish and washed the tools. Inside, she removed her work clothes and lowered them into the washing machine, then she showered to ensure no trace of spray remained before dressing in town jeans, blouse and jersey. She needed to leave the cottage, find fresh air and be as far as possible from Dr Westleigh Thornton!

After banking her wages and wasting time surveying supermarket shelves, she bought a takeaway lunch along with her groceries. The shops were a reminder that she would be on a non-existent budget. The daffodils she had intended to sell were rotting and, even in spring, the flowers which had supported her aunt would be halved. Hazel eyes thoughtful, she wished she had not been quite so quick to reject West's offer of compensation. Her temper had cost her a lot of money. Yet her demand would be expensive for

West and he had warned her it would take time to procure thousands of daffodil bulbs of the quality destroyed. Did she want another paddockful of daffodils?

Amy packed the groceries away in the car and drove towards the beach. Looking at the sea lifted her emotions. There was a soothing quality in the murmurations of the waves, and walking along the sands washed away the traces of anger. A sunwarmed hollow in the sandhills drew her and she spread her rug and sat hidden in the marram grass while she ate her lunch. Three redbilled seagulls observed her, the bravest coming almost within arm's reach and squawking for attention. She thought of Jack O'Day and his delight in chasing the birds. Sectioning off the last sandwich into three, she tossed the scraps out. The beach was suddenly the scene of a dozen gulls squabbling and staking claim and, shaking out her paper, she was amused at their familiarity with human habits as they waddled or flew back to their pursuits. She could imagine West's enjoyment of the incident, his deep chuckle, his mobile, sensuous lips curving back to reveal his white teeth. . .

She stood up and marched back to the car. Included in her groceries was a writing pad and in her purse a pen; she could catch up on some letters while she enjoyed the sunshine. It was a pity she hadn't thought to include her bathing suit and towel; the water attracted but swimming alone could be dangerous. Dismissing the idea, she rolled on some sunscreen and reached for her sunhat, its bright colours faded from summer. The sun's rays were capable of burning and West's comments had ingrained a habit of creaming her skin.

West! No matter what she did or where she went

she could not escape him. In time the ache would
subside, and the best way to lessen the pain was to
think of other things. The daffodils! In a couple of
days the grass would have withered and browned. The
paddock would look barren. Using the two hundred
daffodils she had already removed and another thousand from the second field, she calculated, it would
take her several years to restore the paddock. But did
she want that? Wasn't the destruction a way to force
her to stop and think about her own plans? What had
Aunt Jean often said? 'A new situation, even an
apparent disaster, can be a chance to review and set
goals.'

Hadn't she cherished an idea of establishing a cottage garden, a delight to the senses, where visitors
could discover and buy new perennials and herbs? A
showcase, too, for her skills as a landscape artist. She
had dismissed the plan because of the impossibility of
removing so many bulbs, and the knowledge that the
flowers had been an income for her aunt. The spray
had changed the situation. Half the bulbs had been
destroyed and the remaining half could be shifted to
the woodland area over a period of time. Once she set
out her plans there would be much which could be
done without expense. The rose garden already was a
feature and when she had cleared away the tangle of
weeds and pruned back the shrubs circling it, the area
would be easy to maintain. Throughout the garden
were perennials, including many rare specimens she
had sent her aunt; with time she could nurture them to
productivity. It would be hard work but it would be
enjoyable, and as she gained money from landscaping
she would be able to do more. Long-term she would
have her dream!

Picking up a stick, she moved out to an area of flat,

damp sand where she could etch her plans. As she thought of better ideas or the need for more planting for different seasons, she redrew, using a fresh section of the glistening sand. In the late afternoon she glanced along the beach and laughed at the trail of sketches of herbaceous borders and water gardens, but she was pleased with her efforts. She doodled an extravagant sundial to the formal herb garden and wondered how many years before the sketch became reality. It would all be so beautiful. . .but she needed cash to have some of the heavy work set in place immediately. The water garden she had dug spilled water on her bare feet. The tide had turned, so she ran back to transfer the final sketch on to paper before the incoming waves nibbled her dream away!

Half the pad she spread out in front of her rug-lined nest, each page weighted with miniature turrets of sand. Flat on her stomach, Amy wrote in details of the pump for the fountain by the rock pool. The garden would be a work of art. A gust of warm wind made her look up, surprised to see the sun dipping into the sea. It was time to go home. Her heart missed a beat. Walking along the shore was West and beside him ran Jack O'Day, nose to the sand as if some scent intrigued him. He wouldn't lead West straight to her, or would he?

CHAPTER NINE

WEST sat down on a bleached tree stump. He was staring across the sea and she could read weariness and dejection in his bent back, his hands supporting his head. She yearned to comfort him; it was out of character for West, always so strong and decisive, to be troubled. What was he doing sitting on a beach log? Surely like every kiwi kid he had been told the katipo spider with its poisonous bite could be found on just such a tempting seat?

She watched as he ruffled Jack O'Day's collar, picked up a stick and threw it for him. The action sent Jack skittering, tail pluming, and she was pleased when West stood up to receive the stick and throw it again for Jack. Her relief was short-lived as the pair were headed towards her section of the beach, and she edged back against the sandhill, dismayed when West stopped to study her sketches. Amy persuaded herself her plans would not be recognisable. She gathered her papers, but scent had again attracted Jack's attention. Nose down, he charged in her hidden direction, barking with excitement.

It was no good ignoring his lovable, cuddly dog act. She hugged him, then tried to send him back to West, standing statue-like by her sand drawings. Dismay struck her as she saw West move toward the final plan, its lines partly swallowed by the greedy wavelets. Would it make sense to him?

Jack woofed with impatience and she dismissed West; he was more interested in sand pictures than in what she was doing! With a quick gesture she raced out to the side and Jack rewarded her by circling with happy barks, but she tricked him with a dummy movement and slowed to a dignified walk as they approached West.

'Just returning your dog.' She could hear the splinters of glass in her voice. Jack heard it too and destroyed her composure by snuffling anxiously at her hand.

'He doesn't understand that you are angry with me.'

'Isn't that how you feel about me?' she flared.

'I'm not sure of my feelings where you are concerned. Outraged, disturbed. . . I thought you knew me better. . .but this morning, when you were so upset over the herbicide and the daffodils, you accepted my word when I said there had been a mistake and refused compensation. In the midst of losing half your livelihood, you rescue a worm! You're impossible! Most people would have been plotting to get even, to sue me for as much as possible, but you plan how to salvage something.' He toed the sand map. 'Landscape plans for the cottage? A nursery garden?'

'Yes. West, you don't have to worry about replacement bulbs. Making a garden is what I want to do. It will take me a lot of apple-picking but it will be worth it, and long-term it will advertise my professional skill. The site is grand, the large trees and the cottage are already there.'

'My insurance company will be relieved. I showed them a video I took last year of the bulb fields, so they have an exact picture. Your demand for immediate reconstruction and the problems involved in shifting deep topsoil and trucking in replacement loam to cover several hectares and the difficulty of buying the quality and quantity of bulbs set their computers flashing.

They've offered a lump sum; you should get more than enough to carry out your initial plans and have sufficient left to keep you for a season or two.'

'I don't know what to say. . . I hadn't realised. . .' Yet she should have thought of insurance. 'Thank you, West.' She could see the fatigue in him, and knew he had changed his day to organise assistance for her, the action of a responsible man. She frowned, not wanting to admit it.

'I'd better take Jack O'Day for his run.' He signalled to the dog, his formality an invisible shield. 'The insurance company will contact you.'

'West!' she had uttered his name like a sob on the wind and he turned back, waiting for her to speak. She kicked at the sand, regretting the impulse.

'There is something else, Amy?'

'You know there is! Much more important! Explain about Aroha. I don't understand. She is so like you.' Amy saw West begin to lose the taut grimness in his face.

'You're not accusing me?' He took a step towards her and she felt the power of his eyes searching her. As though satisfied of her sincerity, he began speaking slowly. 'Marty is like me too. When you meet my grandfather, you'll see what I'll look like when I'm seventy. He'll show you a picture of his mother, Aroha's granddaughter.'

'Dominant genes, I got that far. It only confirms the Aroha link.'

'Right! They show up regularly in our families, but the baby is the first in this generation in the Webster clan.'

'I've lost you somewhere!'

'More than a hundred years ago, Aroha was the wife of Tony Webster, a sailor cum farmer-settler and mother of his seven children. When she was widowed, she married my great-great-grandfather and produced three more children.'

'That I didn't know!' She pounced on the fact and surveyed it with care. 'I knew that Aroha had been widowed but not the connection. Now I remember Sue told me Jonathon and Arnold were distant cousins. I'd even thought they were alike in nature!'

'They are. Maybe that's why we all get on so well. The link keeps returning over the generations. Arnold has an aunt Aroha whom many mistake for my mother. She has the same dark eyes and long fingers. She's a florist who manages my shops in Wellington.'

'Kerryanne told me you'd suggested Aroha and that it was a family name, but I thought she meant your family. I didn't realise it was Arnold's family too. When she said Aroha inherited her eyes and fingers from her father, I thought of you. Arnold has blue-grey eyes, but he could pass on the gene.' Amy looked up to see West nod. 'There's something else; why were you rung when Kerryanne went into labour? I suppose there's a reason for that too?'

'Proximity! I live next door. Arnold had arranged to ring me so I'd go over and be there, in case the children woke while he was at the hospital with Kerryanne. The children have known me all their lives, and they trust me, I took charge until Arnold's mother drove out from town early in the morning. Kerryanne's parents died some years ago. Any more questions?'

'No. You have my relieved apology!'

'Accepted!' He smiled. 'But I'm at fault too, I took it for granted you knew the Aroha history. Seeing the baby would have thrown you. She is like me! Very good-looking!' He grinned smugly, then slipped his arms around her. 'That's better! I've been miserable without you, Amy. Keeping busy wasn't enough. I was explosively angry that you could even consider I would be Kerryanne's lover again. You're the woman I want in my life!'

She looked up at him and melted at his expression. He did love her! And she had so nearly thrown away their happiness! She curled herself against him and lifted her lips for his kiss, the quickening warmth at his touch, the surge of desire as his mouth and tongue discovered hers. She was left trembling, hungry for him, knowing his need, but she lifted her head to read his eyes. Dark eyes full of passion and love.

Holding his hand, she led him toward her hidden hollow and lay down on the rug.

'This time I do have protection, Amy. Put them in my pocket the other day and forgot them!' He dropped down beside her. 'You're certain, sweetheart?'

She nodded, very certain that this was her man. His kiss as he acknowledged her was tender and lingering and she almost swooned under its breathless intensity. With a hundred kisses he began undressing her, a button a kiss, a zip, a slide of kisses which tantalised and excited. Her breasts were swollen, her nipples ripe before his fingers caressed them, her loins aching for him as he removed her jeans and knickers. The wind played with her hair as she lay naked.

'I knew you would be beautiful, my Papagena.'

She expected to feel shy, but he was waiting for her and she understood. Lovemaking was a two-way field. Pulling off his jersey was a delicious struggle as he kept nuzzling the closest parts of her body. Shudders trembled through her as she reached his shirt and she had to concentrate on each button until he grew impatient and yanked it off, bruising her with impas-

sioned kisses which threatened their control. He
stopped her and slipped on the condom, wryly admitting further arousal would make it difficult. He kicked
off his jeans and shorts.

'Your skin is so smooth,' he whispered as he drew
her against him. 'So beautiful, my Aphrodite.'

Sensations at his gentle stroking gave way to his
quick thrusting kisses as he laid her on the rug and she
knew his weight and size, their lovemaking urgent in
its rhythm. She was giving herself as she had never
revealed herself before and there was joy, pleasure in
every motion. West was leading her past the clouds,
flying between and above the stars, spinning gold and
silver in a long, magical journey.

The sand was gritty on their skin and she opened
her eyes, surprised it was still daylight. West smiled at
her, his expression tender as he cupped her breasts,
covering her red nipples with shells. Sand trickled
down and West blew the golden grains, making them
dance on her skin.

'You and I are a pair, my Aphrodite. We are shaped
for each other.' He sat up and pulled her against him.

She trembled again as he nuzzled her shoulder.
Facing the sea, she saw it reflect gold. 'Aphrodite was
a creature of the ocean foam! Come on!'

The water was cold, and she went only to her waist
in the water and signalled to West. He plunged to
swim under her, lifting her up, before sliding her down
against his wet body.

'Aphrodite, your cold water unmans me!'

Laughing, she felt his mouth against her own and
the salt water choked them so that they were both
sputtering and clinging together. She felt him wash her
shoulders and breasts and looking down she saw laces
of sea foam on her skin.

'Aphrodite!' he murmured. 'You are mine!'

Backlit by the orange sun he looked magnificent, a primordial man standing in the water. 'Golden man in a golden sea!' Amy let her hands slip down and arched her hips against him while her eyes teased him. She chuckled, tantalising him, knowing she was safe, riding the slow swell of the sea, enjoying the touches and the intimacies as they explored each other. Their kisses grew passionate, the heat of her body had warmed him and she felt him lift her and the aching void was filled by his strength. She heard herself cry out in pleasure. . .she was floating in his arms and he was with her. . .they were together, Aphrodite and her lover, moving in a sea of fire. She felt him move and knew he was carrying her out of the sea, but she was too exhausted to do more than nestle against him as he laid her lovingly on the rug. He was rubbing her dry with his jersey for warmth, frowning as she took so long to respond, but she let him dress her, moving her limbs as needed but unable to contribute more.

'Amy, you nearly made it to Neptune,' he whispered as he wrapped her up. He drew on his shorts and jeans and flung on his shirt then gathered her in his arms.

'I reached Jupiter, I think, West!' she managed before breaking out into shivers.

'No more lovemaking in the sea unless we're in tropical waters!'

'There's always the summertime!' She looked at him sideways.

'We'll get a large spa, my sensuous woman!' West chuckled. 'Practical matters, my bathing beauty. I didn't see your car at the top.'

'If you had you probably wouldn't have come down here! I'm glad I parked it by the far rocks.' She sat up

and made an effort to break the mood of languor
which had covered her. 'I'll go and get it.'

'No, I'll drive you home. While you have a rest, I've
a couple of things to fix up at the lab and I'll send staff
down to pick up your car.' His hand entered her
pocket for the keys and he stopped her protest by
kissing her. 'Later I'll make you a meal and if you're
up to it we can talk things through.'

She nodded and bent to pick up her papers half
buried in the sand. What had she expected him to say?
I love you? Would it have hurt him? But didn't his
tenderness prove how much he cared? Hadn't she seen
love in his star-black eyes?

The wind flicked the rug and sand grains scampered
off. West whistled for Jack O'Day and he appeared
from the sandhills, his head cocked as though disbe-
lieving his play at the beach was over. She walked
beside West, his arm around her, and Jack danced and
pranced ahead of them. With the heater on in the car
she rapidly warmed and when West stopped at the
cottage his dark hair was already drying. She slipped
off his jacket and moved to leave the car, but West
leaned over and kissed her. 'Sure you're feeling all
right, Amy?'

'I'm fine. A hot shower and a drink would improve
matters. You too!'

'I'll have that at the office. I'll be back as soon as
possible, sweetheart.'

Ignoring the browning paddock, she ran inside, her
heart beating in double time. The cottage was still
warm from the heat of the day but she lit the fire, set
the kettle to boil and picked up the next disc from the
pile, read *Othello* and, smiling at the thought of the
love scene, inserted it into the player before running
her shower. After shampooing the salt and sand from

her hair she soaped, rinsed, then hastily dried herself.
The kettle had popped at the boil and she made up
some soup, taking it with her to the bedroom.

She blowdried her hair as she ate her soup, and
decided not to take a rest. The mirror revealed her
glow of warmth and she needed every minute to make
herself beautiful for West. The thought of his tender
compliments made her look for her prettiest undergarments, and she applied her make-up with light touches
before dressing in a slim-fitting black skirt and softly
draped crossover cream blouse. It was an outfit she
had last worn when she had gone out with Jason to a
nightclub in London.

Jason—she had forgotten about him, and as she
checked her appearance she wondered if he had
returned to his home and found work. At least since
she had written her last letter in which she had been
careful to state her lack of love for him, she hadn't
heard any more. She pulled a grimace at her face in
the mirror; she had almost made the mistake of her
life. . . With West there were no fears, only love.

She picked up the towels and went downstairs,
stopping in mid-step at the sight of the tall fair-haired
man who stood in the doorway.

'Jason! What on earth are you doing here?'

'Hello, doll! Can you turn down that screeching?
Can't hear myself think!'

She opened the cupboard, snapped off the sound,
and smiled at his exaggerated rubbing of his ears.

'You look terrific, doll! A knockout! Sorry to surprise but you couldn't hear me call with that music. I
figured you were upstairs so I sat and waited on the
doorstep. Worth waiting for!'

'I wrote to you telling you how I felt. I'm sure you

realise it, now you're home.' Amy spoke with conviction. She saw his backpack in the same moment.

'Sure, doll! But I thought I'd call on you and see if I could change your mind. There is an ulterior motive too. I want to meet the great Dr Thornton, and get a position with one of his nurseries. I wrote to him and sent him a copy of my references and c.v. but his secretary sent back a form letter saying "Thanks, but no thanks"! He probably didn't even see it. I noticed the address "Stone Cottage Road" was next door to yours, so here I am.' He grinned. 'In a small place, like this, you must know him.'

'Yes, of course.' Amy hesitated, wondering if she should explain her relationship with West.

'Don't worry, Amy.' Jason misread her. 'I've already landed a job apple-picking for a few weeks which will give me a chance to suss the local scene, and somewhere along the line I'll meet the man!'

'You've got somewhere to stay?'

'With you?' He smiled. 'I've my sleeping-bag and I'm house-trained! Be neat living with you, so long as you don't play opera all the time.'

'Stay here!' Amy was appalled.

'Look, I won't touch you if that's worrying you. At least, not unless you give me the go-ahead. I need somewhere to doss down, and until I can afford wheels I have to be within pick-up distance in the valley. Your place suits fine; the foreman knew it and he's arranged for someone to call here in the morning. Amy, I promise I'll get out of your hair as soon as I can fix up an alternative. Maybe other pickers will know a place.'

'That's an idea! I haven't even a spare bed! But you can stay in the other bedroom, upstairs. Can you put up with the mattress on the floor?'

'So long as it's warm and dry, I'll be happy. Thanks,

doll. I'm starving, Amy. If you're going out, I can cook myself up a meal.' He thumped upstairs, lugging his pack.

Pondering on other options, Amy heard Jack O'Day's agitated growl at the door. She ran to open it, her heart speeding as West smiled at her. His kiss lingered, teasing her and would have continued but for Jack O'Day's baying and Jason's shouts.

'What. . .?' West was already racing upstairs after his dog. Amy followed with some reluctance but she laughed at the scene upstairs. Jason was protecting himself by standing behind the broken wire mattress and Jack, hair spiked, was uttering low, threatening growls, West holding his collar as though keeping the dog just under control.

Her laughter broke the tension and she made the introductions and brief explanations, but as they trooped downstairs she noticed Jason kept his distance from the dog.

'Dr Thornleigh? You are doing experiments with colour in plants, *Lassiandras*, I believe. I saw the work of one of your colleagues in Holland before I went to London. Glass-house chrysanthemums. I wanted to meet you, but not exactly like this! Always been dead scared of large dogs!'

Amy took Jack beside her and led the conversation into gardens on the Continent, giving Jason a chance to show his depth and knowledge. While they were talking she prepared vegetables, and took a casserole from the deep freeze. Although Jason had suggested she go out, she wanted to make up for his unexpected introduction to West and sharing a meal seemed to be the easiest way to repair the situation. Jack O'Day continued to view the newcomer with hostility, uttering a warning growl if Jason ventured near her. At the dinner-table Jack sat guardian-like in front of Amy's chair.

'He's as much Amy's as he is mine.' West smiled deprecatingly. 'The Irish wolfhound is a fast, loyal creature, bred to attack wolves and protect their owners. Just don't go near Amy, and you'll be all right. No tearing you limb from limb! Besides, I fed him before we came over.'

Amy almost choked on her spinach at the aghast look on Jason's face but she could not allow West to take advantage. 'Relax, West's kidding! Jack O'Day is a playful puppy! Help yourself to some more casserole, there's plenty in the oven.'

It was unfortunate that Jason, taking her at her word, decided to move. A deep-throated growl made him sit down, swearing he'd changed his mind. To Amy, it seemed strange that Jack was behaving so badly, and she looked at West to reprove the dog. A black-eyed sparkle escaped his innocence. He had been signalling Jack O'Day to growl!

Deciding Jason deserved better, Amy led Jack outside, wishing she had taken the action earlier. She wasn't surprised to find Jason was finishing the casserole when she returned.

Pleading fatigue from travelling, Jason retired soon after the washing-up was completed. Before he closed his door, West fetched Jack and settled him on the landing.

'I'll be over to pick up Jack about seven in the morning. He sleeps here. Just keep your door closed and he won't worry you. Goodnight, Jason.'

Amy tried to look severe but giggles convulsed her.

'My darling Amy, if I demanded the right to stay here to protect you from amorous Adonis, you'd be furious with me. Fortunately for me, he's afraid of large dogs! With Jack terrifying him, Jason won't be opening his door till morning. I shouldn't be at all surprised if he finds other accommodation tomorrow.'

West looked so smug that Amy kissed him, her lips tingling with his laughter. She gasped as he found her breasts, unprepared for the passion which flared between them.

'That blouse has been titillating me all evening,' West murmured thickly, his mouth displacing the silken fabric. His hands moved unerringly, dropping her skirt, touching her, and she moaned with the pleasure. She let her fingers slide from the broad plane of his back, worrying at his belt.

'You want me?' West teased.

'You know I do!' She felt him suck in his flat abdomen but it enabled her to undo the belt.

'Pity you've got a house guest!' he mocked softly. 'Jason might interrupt us.'

'And trees grow upside down!'

'So I'm forgiven for terrifying him?' He dropped his trousers and pulled her close. She managed to nod, but then was guided to assist with the condom before he kissed her fumbling triumphant fingers. His smile made the pressure in her loins build to an impossible ache.

'One moment, sweet woman of mine.'

Abandoned, she watched as he flicked on the disc player and he held her as the music filled the room. *Othello*, magnificent, wild with maddened strings of jealousy, love and lust, mingled with their lovemaking, hurting and raising and thrusting, gentle and tender at once. It carried them along and she felt thunder crashing and lightning forking in cataclysmic drama, the music catching them up, bringing them down, only to ride, tortuous and teasing, their senses surrendered to the passion and their bodies united, locked in multiorgasmic movement. When the music released them they were both spent, hurting with exhaustion.

'Woman, I won't be able to move for a week!' West growled after some minutes in which they just lay searching each other. 'Amy, when I'm dying, you'll see me smile and know I am thinking of this time.'

'I never knew lovemaking could be so good and so terrifying at the same time. You were so angry, and so despairing, and just when I couldn't take it any more you would be gentle. . .' She touched his face with infinite care. 'You were always there with the music, you knew every beat, every change of mood. . .'

'*Othello* once meant a great deal to me. I must have played it hundreds of times.'

The story of love, jealousy and tragedy. Amy sat up. 'Melissa!' She felt betrayed.

Stiff, sore, shattered, Amy looked at West. She had thought he was hers, but the music had revealed otherwise. The passion had been much deeper, stronger, a despairing grief—the tender love he had shown had not been for her but for Melissa.

She went to the player and switched off the disc in mid-track then, feeling abused, she entered the bathroom and showered, wrapping the towelling gown around herself. Exhaustion still numbed. When she returned to the kitchen, West had dressed and poured himself a glass of whisky. He offered her one but she shook her head.

'You are the woman I want in my life, Amy.'

'Because you can't have Melissa.'

'She's in the past. You are magnificent. I wanted you, just as you wanted me.'

'I wanted you because I love you. I thought you loved me. My mistake! Stupid, sentimental dreams!'

She had no tears; in his silence, agony walked barefoot on glacier ice.

'Now you understand why I resisted you. But you were always too close to me, and I longed for you. This afternoon I told myself I might not be able to love you, but I could make you happy. Amy, I did believe that.'

She managed to nod.

'Amy, I didn't think this scene would come so soon. I hoped to avoid it.'

'Is she beautiful?' Why did that matter? Why was she tormenting herself?

'Melissa? She has an endearing laugh and soft, gentle eyes. She loved surprises. I never knew what to expect. But her last surprise was too much.' He set down his glass. 'Melissa isn't a strong woman like you, Amy; she couldn't tell me about the children and her husband because she knew it would hurt me.' He managed a dry laugh. 'We send each other cards at Christmas. The ultimate irony!' He turned the crystal glass around and stood up. 'You look pale. It's been a traumatic day. Before you sleep, tell yourself that I did want you, that I do care very deeply for you. Goodnight, Amy.'

Somehow Amy prepared for bed. She ached inside and out as if she had overstretched every muscle, yet it was not the physical pain which caused her distress but the anguish of knowing she did not have West's love. She had been so certain, so convinced of his blanket of love, but there was a handkerchief-sized comfort in the words West had left with her. Repeating them several times helped.

In the morning West came as early as he had promised. He looked so big, so dearly familiar, she could not speak for a moment.

'Good morning, Amy. You are all right?'

She felt his dark eyes study her and knew he saw too much. 'Fine, thank you. Jack is around here, I saw him a moment ago.' She made fists of her fingers to hide their trembling. Abruptly turning back to the kitchen, she saw Jason was trapped halfway down the stairs, Jack growling at the base.

'Jack O'Day! Heel!' West had followed her. Like two innocents master and dog sat down. 'Amy makes excellent coffee!' West poured three cups. 'Sleep well, Jason?'

'Like the proverbial log.'

'Porridge, bacon, egg, tomato and toast! Amy, you sure know how to please a man,' West continued as he passed the pepper and sauce.

Amy looked at West, aware he was playing some agenda of his own. 'There's porridge there if you want some, West.'

'Thanks, sweetheart, and you know how I like my bacon.'

'Well done?' she said with vinegar in her voice as she put another couple of rashers in the pan. Just why West wanted to give the impression they often breakfasted together flummoxed her. If she didn't know better, she would think West was jealous!

West was being paternally solicitous towards Jason as Amy offered West his meal and thumped down the sauce at the same time. 'Don't put it on too thickly!' she warned.

'No, Amy!' Dark eyes danced and his mouth lifted, but he glanced at his watch. 'Your lift should be here in a moment, Jason. Maybe you should wait at the gate?'

Jason finished his tea and, grabbing his jacket, was

gone almost before Amy had finished buttering his toast.

'Would you mind explaining your behaviour, Dr Thornton?'

'Mine, Miss Radcliffe? Just being hospitable!' he chuckled. Seeing her disbelief he shrugged his shoulders. 'Amy, I was just letting your Don Juan know that you are mine.'

'After last night, how can you say that? I am not your woman!' she exploded. 'And I don't want to be the off-course substitute either!'

CHAPTER TEN

'AMY!'

She had turned her back and plunged her hands in the sink but West, standing behind her, put his arms around her and his hands followed hers, gripping her fingers.

'I thought about us during the night. Amy, don't ignore what we do have. We've already achieved something special. We're natural lovers together; both of us are very physical. Deny me, but your body's singing a different song. You're quivering like a reed in the wind.'

'Let me go, West.' She found her hands free as he stepped back. The ache of loneliness replaced his warmth.

'Is that what you really want, Amy?'

Outside two waxeyes were jabbing at insects camouflaged in the bush by the grapevine. She felt exposed, too.

'Aphrodite!' He drew closer and lifted the hair from one ear and blew softly before kissing her neck. 'We have a degree of understanding and honesty which is healthy, and a deep affection and respect for each other. Relationships are not often built on such a solid foundation. I know you love me. I'd like to be able to match your gift but I can't. The best I can offer is that I want to marry you and I would try to make you happy. Think about it.'

The lump in her throat prevented her answer and in

silence she watched as he walked to the door and called Jack from his investigation of the yard.

As he walked away to his boundary her hand went to her neck where West had kissed her. She hadn't expected him to suggest marriage and she tested the thought. Like a leaky boat, at first the advantages appeared solid, but as she investigated the boat took on more water. The telephone interrupted her thoughts and she found it hard to unscramble and recommit her concentration to the insurance officer. He detailed the loss of the bulbs and expressed sympathy before mentioning a sum as compensation. She promised to give the matter consideration and, newly wise, referred him to her solicitor.

As West had suggested, it was a sum sufficient to start work on her garden and by careful management she could live on it for some time. She spent the morning picking some of her harvest of apples and in the afternoon she began checking contour maps of her terrain. If she was to set up her garden, thorough plans were essential. The time passed so quickly she was surprised when Jason was dropped at the gate and realised it was five o'clock.

'I'd forgotten how heavy apples can be!' Jason greeted her. 'The other pickers are a good group, and I've got somewhere to stay. Don't be offended, Amy, it's not you, it's that great silver beast!'

'I'm not in the least offended!' Amy chuckled. 'When do you move?'

'I'll take my gear with me tomorrow morning, if that's OK? Spot levels?' He eyed her papers and equipment. 'I'll wash and give you a hand. Twice as fast with two of us.'

By nightfall they had completed the upper section and Amy was grateful for his help. She had always

known he was an efficient worker and she began to
mull over an idea. Briefly she explained the loss of the
daffodils and the insurance claim and her plans for the
garden. 'So after you've finished the apple-picking
perhaps you could work with me for three weeks? I
should have the plans drawn up and know where I
want to arrange terraces and paths. If a career job
comes up in the meantime, then of course you must
leap for it.'

'Sounds great to me! I'll have another chance to
impress Dr Thornton. He probably thinks I'm the
original twit, being scared of dogs. Mind you, I'm not
so sure I do want to work for him if that dog is around
most of the time. Why didn't you tell me you and the
Doc are an item? I hardly dared glance at you without
those steel eyes of his watching me. I felt like a lad
caught with a hand in the biscuit tin!' He wound up
the line tape as they walked back to the cottage. 'It's a
lovely old place, Amy, you'll make it beautiful.' A
sudden bark spun him round. 'Nemesis!'

'Jack! Where's West?' Her heart thumped so loudly
she was glad Jason had streaked inside. Her fingers
slipped on Jack's neck and she saw Jason's point. She
had not noticed Jack growing, but although not fully
developed he was a big dog. His amber eyes regarded
her playfully and she waited, patting him, as West
drove up.

'Just taking Jack for a run along the beach, Amy.
Come with me? Get your jacket and scarf, the sou-
wester will have teeth out there.'

She nodded, ran inside, informed Jason she would
be back in half an hour and swung up into the wagon.
Jack O'Day sprawled in the rear.

'You've still got your house guest?'

'Till tomorrow morning. I'll be sorry to see him go. Tonight he helped me with the site levels.'

'I could have done that.' West waited for a car then drove on to the road which ran beside the beach. 'Why didn't you ask me?'

'I don't think it entered my head,' Amy admitted. 'You have your own work, and I'm used to doing things for myself. Jason saw me measuring and just started work. He's quick and accurate.' She saw West's mouth tighten and decided not to mention that Jason was hoping for a job. West parked the wagon facing on to the beach and released Jack. Clouds shadowed the grey, metallic water.

'What's your answer, Amy?'

'Without your love, it has to be no, doesn't it?'

'What if I said that no is not a word I find acceptable?'

'Sometimes it has to be said. But it's almost impossible.'

'Remember yesterday? Here on the beach, Aphrodite?'

'Please, don't make it any harder for me.'

'I rather think I'm the one with that problem!' His self-mocking smile caught at her. 'We can talk about it again.' He opened his door and the wind slammed it back. 'It's cold, Amy, perhaps you'd better stay here.'

Amy opened her door and climbed down, the wind stinging her eyes to tears. She wiped them away before West joined her, not wanting to forgo his company.

'Let's run, Amy. Five minutes!'

She took his outstretched hand and began to run, exhilarated by his touch. Hand in hand with West she could do anything! The wind attacking them spat vicious sand grains at their exposed faces. When they

reached the rocks they panted to a halt in breathless
smiles and turned to retreat, slowing to a walk.

'Your cheeks are the colour of sweet red apples!'
West touched her cheek. 'You know I'm hungry for
you. All day I've been thinking about you, Amy.
You're very distracting! I lost one experiment because
I was thinking of the colour of your eyes and I added
the wrong section. Never done anything so stupid!'

Amy tingled, warmed by his admission. If it wasn't
a declaration of love, it bandaged the wound he had
inflicted.

'Jack! Heel!'

Jack had been racing towards a group of gulls, but
one bird had been injured at some time and was not as
fast. West's stern call stopped Jack's game. Reluctance
in every hair, Jack returned, his tail downcast, but a
quick pat and a word from West restored him and he
trotted beside them, head up, tail bannering as they
returned to the wagon. Amy could see parallels with
her own love—without the balance of his love for her,
she was vulnerable. When West opened the vehicle
door for her she clambered in gracelessly, tugging off
her scarf as a defensive manoeuvre as she knew West
wanted to kiss her. She folded the scarf, concentrating
on its precise folds until West shut her door and strode
around to open the rear for Jack. Flapping open and
refolding the scarf occupied her as West took his seat.
Once he started to drive she relaxed, but they were
soon outside the cottage.

'All right, my little hedgehog——' West's smile was
twisted '—your body language is all prickles. Talk is
OK, but not touch!'

'I can't resist you, West. Not if you touch me, you
know that,' Amy admitted, her fingers pleating the
silk again. 'But for me love is important.'

'And sex isn't? Maybe it's just as well I fly north tomorrow. A few days apart should help us.'

'You didn't mention the trip before. Is it unexpected?'

'Yes and no. My flower farm foreman there has taken a lot of time off lately; he's doing his work but something's wrong, I feel it in my gut. . . After talking to him today, I rang the airline. While I'm up north, I'll check the feasibility study regarding the expansion of my shops into the Waikato and Auckland areas. Setting plans in motion, will save me another trip later.'

'If you need staff, think of Jason. He wrote to your company and got the standard form back. He is a good worker.'

'His references were excellent. Sue recognised the name and showed me his file,' West grinned. 'I was tempted to offer him a position in Auckland, just to keep him as far from you as possible! Don't worry, I compromised by asking Sue to find him board, in the valley, where I could keep my eyes on him. As it happens, he found it himself. He has initiative!' West looked at his watch. 'Amy, sweetheart, I've got a lab test due, I'll call back later.'

Amy walked to the cottage, her emotions as gusty as the wind on the beach. Until West had called her sweetheart, she had kept her feelings controlled. She sighed as she opened the cottage door, and the smell of fish and chips cooking greeted her, switching her to the scene. She hadn't even thought about a meal, but her appetite came rushing back!

'Found some fish in the freezer and the potatoes in the bag, Amy. Dinner will be ready in three minutes. Doc not coming?'

'Later. But he won't be expecting a meal.' Amy

hung up her jacket and put the scarf in the pocket. She washed and then helped Jason pile the crisp, golden chips from the paper towels on to the plates. 'Mmm, good!' She risked burning her tongue.

'I counted those!' Jason teased. 'Haven't had any since I left London. Remember the show we went to and afterwards we were ravenous. . .'

'And we went back to my flat and there were about ten people visiting so we had two chips each!'

Talking, laughing, eating, then cleaning up, Amy didn't protest when Jason tuned in some heavy metal on the radio and let the sound blast. She completed her ironing then ran her bath; she could take her time as Jason had showered while she was at the beach. During a long, hot tub she heard the music stop and was not surprised on re-entering the kitchen to find West and Jason having a drink and discussing plants, while Jack O'Day did his hearthrug imitation by the bathroom door. As her heart raced, she strove for normality by patting Jack, but when West's smile touched as he passed her a drink, her hands shook.

The conversation was lively, discussing different gardens, nurseries and floral shows, but at nine-thirty West left to check another experiment. He had entrusted Jack to her—her fridge contained a shelf of dog food—but Amy was disappointed at his casual farewell.

The morning, grey and sulky, matched Amy's mood. Jason, uncertain if he would be picking or not, left at eight with his gear. As she loaded the sheets into the washing machine she heard the telephone ring.

'Amy? Will you drive me to the airport in half an hour?'

'Of course, West. My car hasn't much petrol, but if

we leave five minutes earlier, so I can buy some *en route*. . .'

'We'll take my wagon. It's here.'

'You trust me with it?'

Over his chuckle Amy heard the click as he replaced the receiver. Someone on his staff, if not Jonathon or Sue, could have driven him, yet he had asked her. He wanted to see her! With light steps she danced her way back to the laundry and turned the machine on. Jack raised ears and questioning eyes and she hugged him. 'We're going to take West to the airport. On the way back, if it's not raining, I'll stop along the beach and give you a run.'

Singing Papagena's song, she flew upstairs and applied a little make-up and perfume, untied and brushed her hair, before changing her work shirt for a silk blouse and adding a jacket. Downstairs she took Jack's lead, fastened it, and with him trotting beside her they skirted the brown, dead paddocks and took the short cut to the offices. The receptionist rang through for West and he came out, his briefcase and bag in his hands. Amy drew her breath. Over his suit West was wearing a fine, woollen greatcoat and the long garment accentuated his figure. Underneath the casually open coat his suit's cut and subtle colour was accentuated by the silk tie, revealing the innate style of the man. Jack O'Day bounded towards him but Amy was warmed by West's smile.

'Good morning, Amy.'

'I should have worn a chauffeur's cap! Magnificent!'

Mischief gleamed in his dark eyes. 'Power dressing! A couple of businessmen seem to have the idea I'm a Johnny Hayseed they can manipulate. I could let time prove otherwise, but I've found a meeting can save hassles.'

'I feel sorry for them already!' She took the car key he handed over. 'I'm not sure if I want such an intimidating man watching me!'

'You'll be fine after the first dozen kangaroo jumps!' He opened the door, deposited his bags and Jack jumped into the rear.

'Kangaroo jumps! Ha!' Amy snorted. She tested the gears then started the motor, gaining confidence as she felt its power. By the time she reached the gateway she was at ease and aware of West's approval. When they arrived at the airport, she parked neatly. 'Fun! I'll drive this machine any time! Consider a swap with a venerable model hatchback with more than its share of rust?'

'You'd be angry with me if I bought you a car, even though I worry about you in that wreck. Jason left this morning?'

'Yes. I shall miss him.'

'I wanted to see you before I left. To apologise. I behaved like a jealous husband, but I had no right. I'm sorry.'

Amy's fingers tightened on the steering-wheel, bracing her arms like buttress supports for her body as she struggled to rationalise his apology. Her throat thickened and she swallowed the lump of hurt. 'Forget it. Haven't you a plane to catch?'

'Yes. There's no need for you to waste any more of your time. Thanks for bringing me. Use my car while I'm away. No? Give the keys to my receptionist.'

In the mirror Amy saw him hesitate, but he patted Jack, then opened the door and moved out, retrieving his cases before he turned back to her.

'You won't accept anything I can give, and I can't offer what you want. Goodbye, Amy.'

His quiet formality appalled her. This was the end

of her dreams? In a grey tarsealed car park, compartmentalised by white geometric strips, separate identities going in their own directions? Yet hadn't it been her decision? Amy started the engine and reversed from the parking space. Concentrating on driving, she didn't allow herself the luxury of examining her hurt until she reached the beach.

Walking along the strip of shore, Jack trotting eagerly ahead on his tour of inspection, Amy acknowledged West's point. The thought caused an ache, the weight in her chest a manifestation of grief. West had accepted her refusal. Honesty compelled her to admit that she had told West not to touch her. He had wanted to carry on their intimate relationship, he had offered to share his life. Why couldn't she accept?

Jack's barking attracted her attention and she saw the lame gull backed against a sand dune. The bird, squawking an indignant protest, made small awkward runs, beak an attacking ram, keeping Jack at a distance.

'Jack, come! Heel, boy!' Amy called, guilty that in her self-absorption she had not noticed Jack's action. As he ran back to her, the hunched gull squawked another insult and she smiled at its spirit. Despite its handicap, or perhaps because of it, the bird had learnt to protect itself. There was a parallel—unless West loved her as she loved him, both of them would be handicapped.

She lectured Jack about the responsibility of preserving freedoms as they walked back along the sand and Jack, ears cocked, knew she was talking more to herself than to him, but his golden eyes were sympathetic. At the hollow where West and she had made love, she broke into a run, unable to meet her thoughts. Jack O'Day raced ahead and neither stopped until they reached the wagon.

Over the following days, rain and wind stopped her from doing work in the garden, but she kept busy by lifting the old linoleum in the cottage kitchen, bathroom and laundry. Underneath the layers the wide rimu floorboards were only slightly marked, making her plans of 'distressing' them with a lime wash practical. Removing the old tacks took hours on her knees and in a few places the holes gouged out had to be filled, but after sanding the boards with hired equipment she achieved an excellent surface. Sue and Jonathon visited and Amy had basked in their approval of her meticulous work, and she had been pleased when Jonathon had trucked out the pile of old lino. Their reminder of the ball at the end of the week disturbed Amy. She hadn't heard from West, but Sue told her he had negotiated an excellent lease agreement for three shops in Auckland and two in the Waikato, and was working through plans for supply with his Auckland manager.

Amy's new-found peace eroded at the thought of the ball, uncertain whether West still expected her to go. She wasn't sure she could cope with dancing with West. So long as they did not meet, she could manage one day at a time, especially when each day involved penitential positions as she began lime washing the floor with neat, even strokes. When it was finished she was thrilled with the result; the faint blue note to the boards enabled the timber to be seen and gave her the exact blue-grey colour to pick up in the wildflower curtains she purchased. She was finishing hooks in the new curtains when the telephone jarred her. West's deep voice was enough to make her heartbeat speed.

'Amy! It's been a long time. I hear the weather has

held up the garden plans. How's Jack O'Day? Behaving himself?'

'He's fine. It's a wonder he hasn't a grossly distended stomach—he keeps trotting to the orchard to eat the apples! We've just come back from a run along the beach. Jack's finally learnt he's not allowed to chase seagulls.' West's low chuckle in her ear was erotic and she tightened her fingers on the receiver.

'I tried ringing you earlier. I had intended to be home today, but I can't make it until tomorrow night. Sorry, Amy, but I won't be with you at the ball before ten. Sue and Jonathon have said they would be happy to pick you up for dinner at seven-thirty. They will look after you.'

'Tell them not to worry. I wasn't sure whether you wanted to go with me. I'm quite happy staying home. . .'

'You love dancing and I want to dance with you!' There was a slight pause. 'Look, why don't you ask Jason? Presumably golden boy can dance!'

Amy closed her eyes, shutting out the pain. How could West, knowing how much she loved him, suggest she go with another man? Hadn't he bought her the red rose gown?

'Jason's mother runs a school of dance. He's won prizes here and in Europe.' There was tartness in her tone. 'We used to dance in London, he taught me a lot.'

'Fine! I'll see you there. Goodnight, Amy.'

The connection clicked off and she replaced the receiver. Stiff-shouldered, she marched across the room and switched off *The Magic Flute*. She had been stupid to play it: the opera was inextricably linked to West. Jack, sensing her misery, snuffled at her fingers. 'I have to forget all the emotional baggage!' she told

Jack as she patted him. 'But I don't know how to dump all the contents!' Jack walked over to the refrigerator. 'Priorities! Right? As far as you're concerned, number one is food!'

She fed him, let him outside and then ran her bath. The telephone rang soon after she had climbed in, but she ignored it and the summons stopped, leaving a loud, accusing silence. Irritated, she wished she had thought to switch it off. She soaped, scrubbed and splashed, but the echo of the unanswered call stayed with her. Instead of enjoying her tub, she clambered out clean, but not relaxed. When Jack returned and plonked himself down in front of the pot-bellied stove, she reached for his brush, her mood calming as she brushed his silver hair. It was more wiry, but shone with good health and daily brushing. The telephone rang again and she grabbed at it.

'Hi, Amy! Jason. I hear there's a ball at the Community Centre and that Doc Thornton is held up, so you need a partner for dinner and the first dance. Would you allow me to escort you?'

'Jason, that's good of you. How did you hear?'

'Ha! Old trick! Place ear to ground. Listen with care. Look first, in case owner of ear coming!'

Despite her earlier bleak mood, Amy laughed.

'Dr Thornton rang me a few minutes ago. His foreman up there has just undergone medical tests and the results will be back tomorrow, so he promised to stay until then. He was concerned about letting you down—his flight doesn't link up until late, then he has to go home to change.'

'So you agreed?'

'Of course! It pays to do one's boss a favour!'

'Your boss?'

'Temporarily. He's offered me a job for three

months, assisting the foreman up there. If I prove myself, and I will, Doc's promised me a career position within the firm. Apparently you told him I was a good worker. Thanks, Amy! I owe you one!'

'Consider the debt paid when I step on your toes!'

They arranged details for the evening before saying goodnight. The knowledge that West had asked Jason to look after her until he arrived made up for the earlier hurt. Upstairs Amy took out the glowing red gown, warmed by its richness. She looked in the mirror, the red dress pretty, but the sadness in her eyes giving her away. Perhaps tomorrow, when they danced, mightn't West fall just a little in love?

Scorning her hopes, she rehung the dress and ran downstairs, deciding that hooking the curtains made more sense. In the morning the faded wallpaper seemed even more dingy when she had hung two of the new curtains. Indecision hovered for a moment then she rang the solicitor and was informed the insurance company had paid in the cheque. Pleased she had put a deposit on the wallpaper, she took down the two curtains, carried them with care into the front room, and, returning to the kitchen, she reached for an edge of the old wallpaper. With a laugh, she tugged and it tore, racing up the wall to the ceiling.

Jason's arrival after breakfast was a surprise; he was bored because the weather had delayed the picking and his chance to earn money. Employing him to help with the stripping made the task much more fun, and by afternoon tea they had only one more small wall to complete.

'We should stop here and clean up the mess. There's the ball tonight,' Jason reminded her.

'But we'll soon have it finished!' Amy pleaded.

'Slavedriver! If your escort arrives late, blame yourself!'

It was almost six before the wall was stripped and, guiltily aware of the time, Amy loaned Jason the car so he could go home to shower and change. She bagged up the ripped-off pieces and swept the floor before she could let Jack O'Day inside. Feeling as if she had been rolling in dust, Amy showered, shampooed and conditioned her hair, enjoying the spray of warm water.

As she went upstairs, she wondered if she could face the evening. How could she be strong when West danced with her? Somehow she would have to avoid the last dance, make sure that, like Cinderella, she left alone before the ball was over.

Her car! Jonathon had confirmed he would pick them up, but she would ring and explain she was running late and would meet them at the restaurant. After the ball she would have to drive her car home— sanity would have a chance if she were separated from West. A glance at the clock told her she would not be telling lies. She pressed the buttons and an agitated Sue, confessing she was only half dressed, sounded grateful for the extra minutes. Amy, looking at her damp towel, decided not to reveal her lack of even a half, and sped to the bathroom to throw on her wrap and returned to the kitchen to feed Jack.

Blowdrying and fixing her hair took time and she was appalled to see Jason drive in as she finished the stockings, petticoat and make-up stage. She slipped on her red dress, high heels and ruby earrings. The woman who stared back from the mirror startled her. Extra make-up had made her eyes seem larger, her skin tone enhanced by the red gown. Twirling, she saw the flow of the fabric as she moved, revealing her figure from the long line of her leg to her creamy shoulders and fine neck. The smooth, upswept style of her hair gave elegance. She was beautiful! The new insight gave her a trumpet of confidence.

Jason's wolf-whistle as she ran out to the car made her laugh—she was going to enjoy herself! At the restaurant, when they entered, there was a silence, as if everyone in the room had stopped, like a filmclip, then been edited into motion. Jonathon came forward with glasses of pale gold sparkling wine, and she introduced Jason.

'My brother is either very trusting or crazy, letting this spectacularly beautiful woman out with you!' Jonathon shook Jason's hand. 'Come and meet everyone else.'

The rest of the group were having drinks, making introductions easy, and the compliments at her appearance thrilled Amy. The manager presented her with a long-stemmed red rose which West had sent. The gesture made her smile wobble.

'Isn't love grand?' Sue teased *sotto voce*. 'Jonathon and I are really happy about you and West. The ideal couple! Every day when West rings he always asks me about you, but Jonathon wouldn't let me tell him about your improvements to the cottage. He claims it's your nesting instinct at work and would be a surprise for West!'

'Disillusion him, just the weather keeping me indoors and the insurance money enabling me to make a start.' Amy twinkled with her new, inner strength. As they moved into the restaurant proper and were shown to their places, she was aware of Jason's protective care. 'I'm just the sturdy Mrs Mop of this afternoon!'

'No, you're not!' Jason surveyed her. 'You're the

scarlet woman, beautiful and dangerous. . .my future boss should be warned that every man in this room wants to seduce you!'

'Don't tell him, let him find out for himself!' Amy chuckled. The thought was over the top like the bubbling wine. 'Let's dance, there will be time before our orders are ready.'

The music was from a trio of players and already several couples were dancing. Slipping into step with Jason, Amy enjoyed the melody, and when the dance ended and another began they left the floor with reluctance as the food for their group was being set. The meal passed at a leisurely pace, Amy danced with others between courses, and by the time they were ready to go to the ball, the flattery had gone to her head more than the glass of wine. If West couldn't fall in love with her, it was his loss, wasn't it?

CHAPTER ELEVEN

AT the Community Centre the hall was artistically decorated with flowers and ferns and groups of tables clustered together. Their party grew lively and a Latin American number made Amy's toes tap and she smiled at Jason. 'Where's your heavy metal now?'

'Same place as your opera! Let's dance!'

The music encouraged, enticed, then became bold. Amy followed Jason step for step. As the music sped, the challenges of the dance opened out and Amy was aware of the crowd stopping to admire, then clapping in time from the circle of the floor. Faster and faster, the intricate movements led to the climax with a flourishing dramatic pose. As the applause washed them, she curtsied an acknowledgement, the moment giving time to ease her panting breath.

As she stood, she saw West. He was clapping too as he stood at the doorway, magnificent in his dark evening suit. Without thinking she ran to him and his smile, tender and possessive, rewarded her.

'You are beautiful, Amy.'

Others had said similar things but it was West's words which wrapped her in happiness. With his arm around her, guiding her forward, she held out a hand to Jason, apologising for darting off so abruptly. They walked over to the table together and the group encircled them, welcoming West and praising the dancers. While West was getting a drink, Amy slipped into the powder room to check her appearance, recombing her hair into place and cooling her flushed face. As she returned, West led her on to the dance floor. Jason introduced her to another young woman and their foursome swapped, changed and laughed to the pounding beat of a revived rock number. The next dance she shared with Arnold, while Kerryanne and West danced together, and the following number she enjoyed with Jonathon. She sat out another dance, talking with some new friends, with West; some of their group were leaving and Amy was astonished to note it was after one-thirty. West offered her a drink.

'No, thanks, West, I have to drive home.'

'I'll take you, Amy. Jason mentioned he would like to take home the woman he met, but he lacked a car. In the interests of romance, I gave him permission to take yours. He has the keys.'

West's smile devastated her intentions. From the doorway Jason waved an acknowledgement, and seeing his wink meant solely for West added to her indignation.

'I owed him a favour,' West murmured, his dark eyes laughing.

'You pair of schemers! Jason was my friend!'

'He is! But he's a man who wants a certain job.'

'That's manipulation! Gross!'

'I agree. Shameful! Our dance, Rose Red!'

It should have been easy to refuse him, but his smile held tenderness and she yearned to dance with him, the band playing a slow, romantic number Amy could not resist. Stiff at first, she softened with the music, allowing West to draw her closer until she relaxed when the lights lowered, and closed her eyes. She drifted with West, aware of the shifting strengths of his muscles, the rest provided by his shoulder for her head, the woven silk and wool texture of his dinner suit and, snuggling close to his lawn shirt, she could smell his clean, fresh body scent. West's hands pressured her hips fractionally and her footsteps missed a beat. She lost the music when West kissed her shoulder and raised her face to kiss her lips briefly. They were by the door and she did not protest when he led her outside. His kiss tasted her lips, teasing the fullness in her lower lip then, at her tremor, he deepened the intimacy, blasting away the remnants of her control.

'Sweetheart, thoughts of you have driven me mad,' he muttered as he nuzzled her ear. 'I've never wanted anyone as I want you. You torment me, day and night. Forget what I said the other morning. I've tried to respect your wishes, but every fibre in me protests. I wouldn't contact you until I had to last night. . .but everywhere you were with me, at every decision I found my judgement tempered by yours. Each of us is tuned like a Stradivarius to the other. We're so right together!'

She opened her full lips and smiled up at him. His words sounded very like a declaration of love! Standing on tiptoe, she reached his mouth and teased it open, her hands holding him, her fingers lifting and stranding his dark hair. Releasing his mouth, she drew kisses along his shadowed beardline.

'We'll go and say goodnight to the others.' His voice was deep.

'There's an after-ball party we were invited to attend.' Earlier she had been pleased with the invitation, but regretted having to mention it.

'Make our excuses,' West murmured as he smoothed her dress back into shape on her shoulder. 'I'll just visit the men's room.' Glad the dim lights did not reveal her lips so obviously kissed, Amy re-entered the hall and walked back to collect her bag from the table. The sensation that something was wrong in the depleted group hit as Sue crossed to meet her.

'Amy, I have to speak to West. Do you know where he is?'

Amy explained and saw Sue wordlessly signal Jonathon.

'Sue? What is it? Trouble? At the office? The glass-houses?'

'It's not that simple.' Sue drew the words with reluctance. 'I think West will have to tell you.'

It seemed an hour before the two men returned. Amy knew it was less because the band had only played one song. A gaunt-faced West strode towards her.

'Sorry to keep you waiting, Amy, I'll take you home now.'

Amy intercepted his glance but he looked away on the pretence of wishing the others goodnight. His action chilled. She said her farewells with dignity and walked beside him to the wagon. He opened the door for her, tucked in her dress and closed the door. Amy sat silent as he drove straight to the cottage, his lips compressed, knuckles white on his hands on the wheel. Familiarity with the moonlit scene told Amy every-thing at the flower farm appeared normal. Only some-thing powerful could have shocked West, and dismayed Sue. Something or someone. Instantly Amy guessed the truth. She braced her shoulders as West stopped the vehicle.

'Amy, I don't know how to tell you.'

'Melissa?'

'How did you know?'

'Intuition. Something is wrong with Melissa's hus-band? She's free now?'

'I don't know yet. She just arrived at the farm.'

'Melissa's here?'

'I can't believe it myself! With the two boys. Out of the blue! Sue's cousin who is the babysitter rang the Centre for me, but we were outside and Jonathon took the call.'

Amy wrenched open the door, sharp with distress. 'You'd better go. You can't have Melissa and her two children wandering around, jet-lagged and exhausted at two o'clock in the morning.'

Somehow Amy left the vehicle and walked to the cottage. As she went inside and switched on the light, she heard the wagon motor start. West was going to the woman he had loved so long. Amy leaned against the door, energy ebbing. Jack O'Day looked up, but made no attempt to move from his sheepskin mat. Amy knew she should move, but wasn't sure if she could. She felt frail, like an invalid. Gripping the table, she breathed deeply, concentrating on not fainting. Her clothes were suddenly restrictive and she kicked off her high-heeled shoes and removed the red dress roughly. With effort she performed her nightly ablutions and propped the door open for Jack, as she didn't want to have to let him out in a few hours' time. It was cold standing in the doorway in her petticoat and stockings, her skin goosebumping and turning blue.

Upstairs she sat shaking and shivering on her bed. Even to bend to remove the stockings required effort. There was a hole in her new stockings at the toe line; she dropped them and they formed a puddle on the carpet. She tugged off the rest of her underwear, pulled on her nightgown and climbed into bed. The warmth of the electric blanket soothed and she switched it and the light off and lay staring at the battened ceiling.

Incidents flickered—the red dress, the restaurant,

the gift of the rose, the ball, the triumphant dance, the joy in looking up to see West, his smile loving and tender as she ran to him, the pleasure in dancing with him, their completeness with each other. Amy sighed. For a few moments love had united them. Turning over and pulling the duvet around her to comfort, she pondered how his love, which had developed from their frequent meetings, their shared interests, their natural attraction, could be frosted, like a tender plant.

Wasn't there hope in that he had wanted to tell her the new development before seeing Melissa? He had not suggested that Jonathon and Sue take her home. There was no pretence; he hadn't lied to her. What if the meeting with Melissa forced West to realise that his love for her had withered away? That all he had left was a memory. Could it be the breakthrough where he acknowledged that he loved Amy Jean Radcliffe?

When Amy woke, Jack O'Day was snoring beside the bed. She eyed him, wondering if his master was sleeping just as deeply, then glanced at the bedside clock radio. Most of the morning was gone! Frowning, she looked at the undergarments on the carpet and remembered her shock of the previous night. Overnight she seemed to have slept her way to acceptance of the situation. If West loved her and she loved him, Melissa's arrival was only going to clear away some weeds from the garden of their love. All she had to do was wait, and she was not going to sit around and fret.

Downstairs she cooked toast and tomatoes and decided to go into town to buy the wallpaper and paint. As she finished her toast she remembered her car had been loaned to Jason. A check outside the door showed he had returned it, but the keys were absent. Under the windscreen he had left a note:

Thanks for a great evening. Nemesis is growling every time I go near the gate, so I can't leave the keys, though the door is open! I'll take them over to Doc's office. Jason.

Amy screwed up the note and flung it into the pot-bellied stove; the idea of going across to the office and meeting Melissa appalled her. Gratefully she remembered the spare key and ran upstairs. In town she parked in the shop's car park and went directly to the wallpaper counter. A short time later she emerged with paint, brushes, size, paste, sandpaper and a bundle of wallpaper. It had added up to more than she had expected, but the colour-matching had been exact and it had kept her thoughts from West and Melissa for minutes at a time.

As they passed the beach she couldn't ignore Jack's pleading whine, and she stopped the car. The sou-westerly was blowing straight from Antarctica and, as she ran with Jack, it was impossible not to remember how West had held her hand and smiled, calling her windstung cheeks sweet red apples. Breaking the thought, she angled her way, zigzagging to avoid the wind and extend Jack's run. His golden-eyed excitement as she changed step rewarded her and she kept it up until the last twenty metres when they raced for the vehicle. Back at the cottage she put on old gear, mixed size and then washed down the kitchen's ceiling and wooden cupboards. She had finished the chore and sat down to enjoy a mug of coffee when her heart missed a beat at the click of the rear gate. Her bravery crumpled, yet she had known West would pick up Jack O'Day. With relief she heard Sue's call.

'Come in! Coffee's just made.'

'Love a mug. I had to come and see you, Jonathon and I were concerned for you.'

'I'm glad it's you and not your brother-in-law! I've got to go next door and I've been putting it off. . . Jason left my car keys there. I don't suppose you have them?'

'Sorry! I'll get them for you later. The place has been chaotic; West brings more orders every time. Usually he's so efficient, but this morning he was absent-minded and contrary.'

'He's not happy?'

'Far from it! Jonathon thinks West idealised Melissa and the reality won't live up to his memory. Their relationship was short-lived. If it had been given time, it might have faded naturally. From the beginning Jonathon was appalled by Melissa's failure to tell the truth, and he wondered why she was staying at a luxury resort when she had a husband and two pre-schoolers at home. He said to tell you to keep smiling. But it's easy to give advice!'

'I'm trying to keep busy. My panacea!' Amy gestured to the room. 'I keep wondering where they are, what is happening, why she came. . .?'

'It appears to be a spur-of-the-moment decision. At first I was sorry for her—she had an argument with her husband over money, so she took the two children out of school, and drove to the airport. They had a three-hour wait for the flight to Wellington. She didn't mention she was aiming for Nelson, so no one told her there were flights to Auckland and Christchurch with connecting links. Instead of returning home to pack some clothes they sat and waited, abandoning the car in the car park. When they arrived in Wellington she found out the last flight to Nelson had left. Most people would have booked accommodation then, but she had one object in mind: to reach West. The booking clerk told her of the ferry and arranged a rental car at Picton. Melissa dragged the boys along for a three-and-a-half-hour trip across Cook Strait, took the rental car and at eleven o'clock at night set off to drive here, up and down hills and round the Sounds for miles! At two in the morning she arrived here, fraught and shivering, the boys had thrown up everywhere, and she didn't have a clean stitch for any of them.' Sue shook her head. 'I've been trying to make excuses for her, but blaming the full moon seems the most charitable! She called it a surprise for West!'

'He wasn't the only one she surprised!' Amy poured Sue another cup, but her hand was not steady.

'Last night you and West were so happy. Jonathon and I both agreed that West had finally forgotten Melissa, and like the bad fairy she turned up. Now that I've met her, I can't see them as a pair. Melissa sobbed all over him and the white-faced boys smelt revolting and they whined non-stop. Poor little beggars. I found them some pyjamas and an outfit for the morning and packed them off to shower and change. Melissa spoke about staying with West; she was almost hysterical when I said they could stay with us as West had a one-bedroomed flat! Hissed at me that she'd found out, a week ago, that West was a multimillion-aire and that I was a lying, obstructive female. She didn't realise West was behind her. The look on his face when he apologised to me and said he'd arrange a hotel suite in town! While he telephoned, she wept all over him, saying she wasn't rational because she was exhausted. That I believed! As the boys returned from the shower, Jonathon and West wrapped them in blankets and tucked them into the back seats of our ute. West tailed him with Melissa and the rental car, and at the hotel Jonathon and he carried the boys to the suite. When Melissa tried to detain West, he told her that she was in no state for discussion, and he would contact her late afternoon.' Sue grinned. 'Hardly the eager lover!' She glanced at her watch. 'I'm telling you all this because you have West's interests deep in your heart. I could be wrong, but I fear Melissa's are deep in West's pockets.'

After Sue's departure, Amy began sloshing size on the kitchen walls, trying desperately to think of anything other than West and Melissa. As she began the third wall, Jack's excitement warned her of West's approach and she had time to wash her hands.

'Come in, West. You're here for Jack?'

'Partly. Your keys. I came over earlier but you were out, so I knew you had a spare set.' His long fingers played in Jack O'Day's silver hair. 'I missed you, fella!'

'I'll get his lead. He had a run along the beach before lunch.'

'Amy. I wanted to see you.'

'Why?' Standing straight and tall, forcing her knees back hard so the tension would help maintain an apparent calm, Amy handed him the lead and the bag containing Jack's brush.

'When I was away, I'd find I was thinking about you.' West spoke slowly. 'About us.'

'But now you have Melissa.' She kept her voice steady.

'It wasn't the fantasy I'd dreamt about years ago.' West's mouth curved into the familiar, self-mocking smile. 'More a nightmare! I can't imagine what Melissa was thinking about to inflict such a journey on her sons.'

'People react differently to stress.' Her hands were trembling so much she laced her fingers together.

'Amy, the last thing I want is to hurt you. But I'm unsure about my feelings.'

She shook her head as he moved to hold her. 'No, don't touch me, leave me alone. I want to keep busy.'

West stepped back, dropping his hands to his sides. 'It looks as if you have been! You've done something to the floor, it feels different.' West toed the newspaper covering the floor and bent to admire the surface. 'Amy, this is wonderful, the original timber with a lime wash treatment.' He shifted some more newspaper and inspected the floor. 'I always wanted to have that done. It's come up well. The tradesman made an excellent job.'

'I should have started with the ceiling and worked down. Until I finished the floor, I didn't realise how much the rest of it irritated. It's been too wet and windy to garden.'

'*You* did it? Fantastic!'

'Jason helped me strip the walls yesterday. The wallpaper's over there. I was pleased with it.'

West inspected one of the rolls. 'Good choice. Right design for the style of the cottage. Have you organised a paperhanger?'

'I thought I'd try; my flatmate and I put some up a couple of years ago.'

'When I was a student I did some—it's not one of my favourite tasks! Unfortunately, I'm days behind in my own paperwork, but I'll see what I can do.'

'I can manage.' Her effort to be strong was running out. 'Thanks for returning my keys. I'd like you to leave now.'

He accepted the dismissal, nodded and walked out of the door, Jack O'Day bounding in front. As she sniffed back the tears, Amy brushed on the size, the regular rhythm assisting in keeping her emotions under control. It was ten o'clock when she finished the work and wearily climbed the stairs. Twenty-four hours earlier she had seen West, tall, distingushed in his dinner suit, and she had run to greet him and seen the tender pride in his dark eyes. She had been so sure of his love, but Melissa's arrival had challenged everything.

In the morning, sunshine cheered her and she left the doors wide open to air the cottage, then barrowed a pile of empty boxes up to the orchard and began picking and packing the apple crop. Jack O'Day appeared, tail wagging, eyes bright, and he settled to crunch some of the windfalls. Amy looked for West, relaxing when he was not in sight. After midday she hefted two of the full boxes on to the barrow and began pushing them down towards the shed, arriving in time to see an unfamiliar van edging out of her gateway. Lowering the barrow, she ran across the lawn hoping to read the number plate. 'Some guard you turned out to be, Jack, but I left the doors open, inviting a burglar. . .' Fear accused as she raced inside. The kitchen glowed.

'Someone's put up the new paper. It looks great!' She wrinkled her nose against the odour of damp paper and paste. A tradesman's card and guarantee of workmanship had been left on the table. 'West! Only you would have arranged this!' she told Jack.

Amy made a pot of tea and walked round, cup in hand, admiring the butted joins and the finishing frieze. With the wooden ceiling she had washed days before and the newly limed floor, the kitchen delighted her. It was tempting to hang the new curtains but the paper was not quite dry and she reminded herself that there were full boxes to cart downhill and store, and more apple trees to harvest. West's gesture reinforced her love, and she found hope in knowing that he had considered her and wanted to help with the cottage, despite Melissa's arrival.

She smiled as Jack seized a runaway apple as his prize.

'You and I'll never be able to eat so many! Wonder what Aunt Jean did with them all? Even if I made a pile of apple chutney and apple pulp. . .what do you say, Jack? Give some away?'

She made a ploughman's lunch of bread and cheese and ate it sitting on the garden seat, mentally doodling other improvements. West's suggestion of the architect sympathetic to the style was a practical one, but it would have to wait until she knew her earning power — the garden venture offered difficulties as well as possibilities. Attentive sparrows, warily eyeing Jack's pose as a rug, disposed of the crumbs and she tossed them the last piece before taking her plate and cup back to the kitchen bench. Colour schemes for the two upstairs bedrooms kept her mind occupied as she picked more apples. When she had barrowed the last box for the day, she entered the kitchen with pleasure. The paper had dried and only a hint of the smell remained.

She ran her bath, piled in perfume oil and left the bathroom door open for the scent to permeate the kitchen. Deliberately she chose *The Magic Flute*. Papageno, as well as the Prince, had found difficulties on the search for love and there was comfort in the story. A long soak restored her aching muscles and she riffled through her drawers and wardrobe for something pretty to celebrate the new décor. After striping burgundy polish on her toenails, she brushed her hair and plaited a burgundy silk scarf through it. She slipped on a white broderie anglaise petticoat,

covered it with a blue top and matching skirt, and
deepened her burgundy toned lipstick. It was, she
decided, daft to dress up to match a kitchen, but it had
amused her and stopped her from thinking of West
and Melissa for a few more moments. At the thought
of them together, she was in agony. What if West did
love Melissa?

Chilled, Amy went downstairs, her feet dragging.
Images of West and Melissa making love were fluores-
cent flashes, dazzling and darkening, luminous and
lowering, a disco lightshow which left Amy shaking
and pale. She ran out to the garden, startling a
blackbird which shrieked an alarm. The sound pulled
her up short, and she forced herself to look at the
moonlit garden, breaking the terrifying imagery. A
late perennial had flowers in bud and, surprised, she
identified the former small plant of love-lies-bleeding.
The appropriately named plant's success gave her
courage, and she went inside with more calm and
began making a meal. While it cooked, she began
hanging the first curtain and after she had eaten and
tidied the kitchen she resumed hooking and hanging
the rest. The task was enjoyable as each set finished
off a wall, and she was eager to fit the last one on the
high window by the stairs. After readjusting the
ladder, she was halfway through when West's distinctive knock set her heart racing. With Jack outside, she
had not heard West arrive. What if he had brought
Melissa? Wobbling, she climbed down, breathed
deeply, put on her moccasins, and straightened her
body for the blow. Had West come to tell her he
intended to marry Melissa as soon as the divorce went
through? It took all her courage to open the door. He
was alone.

'West!' Her voice had a raw edge.

'Can I come in? I wanted to see——'

'The wallpapering! It's wonderful! Such a surprise!' She was grabbing at words like a conjuror, trying to stop him from telling her of his proposal.

'It looks great, Amy. I was worried you wouldn't approve of my calling in an expert, but I couldn't have made such a neat job and it would have taken me days! Let me help with the last curtain?'

'I can manage, thanks.' Amy kicked off her moccasins and scrambled up the stepladder to get away from him. She perched on the top and pulled the curtain to her.

West frowned. 'You're taking a risk.'

'I'm fine!' Amy swung her legs to show confidence then wished she hadn't. West's mouth twitching smile told he appreciated the display of broderie anglaise petticoat and smooth, bare legs and feet.

'Very fine!' he murmured as he moved to stand beside the ladder. 'All the same, I'll hold it for you.'

West's mouth on a level with her toes made her very conscious of him; she had never thought of her feet as erotic objects before and tried to hide one behind the other.

'Striped toenails!' His fingers tickled her toes gently.

Her normally deft fingers stubbed at mating hook and ring as she tried not to reveal her rising sexual tension. She fixed the last one into position and smoothed out the curtain.

'Perfect!' West admired.

Amy glanced down, sensing his words had nothing to do with curtains, but his smile teased. She backed, toes feeling for the rungs. Halfway down West gripped her waist and lowered her feet to the floor.

'I couldn't resist any longer. You have the sexiest toes I've ever seen! That enticing petticoat. . .'

Amy escaped. 'Don't. . . Melissa. . .'

'Forget her! It's just you and I, my darling.' He dropped a kiss on her fingers.

Amy looked at him wide-eyed, barely able to take in his words.

'I've been an addlehead, sweet Amy. You entranced me almost as soon as we met. I'd brainwashed myself that I couldn't love again, that Melissa was my perfect woman. . .but now I know better. Apparently, a week ago, she'd read an article in a magazine about me, so she decided to rekindle the flame. Last night she set up the dinner and candlelight scene. All she would talk about was my money, my shops, my income! I punished her by lecturing her on the genetic coding in flowers. She tried to keep smiling, but by the time dinner was over her pretty pansy expression was artificial. Then I announced I had an experiment to check and I had to leave. I drove home, checked the plant, and Jack and I went for a long run to the beach and back. The cold night made me a little clearer and I kept thinking of your shining integrity, generosity and gentleness.'

Amy sat down, very suddenly. West moved to the window beside her seat.

'This morning I knew I had to resolve the situation, so I invited her to bring the boys to see the office and the plant after work. Fortunately, Sue and my secretary stayed on. I showed Melissa and the boys around, and left them in my outer office for a few minutes, as I had to take a call. When I returned, Melissa and I heard Sue reprimanding the elder boy; he'd gone into her office, played with the computer, reducing pages to blanks. If there hadn't been a back-up, that game would have cost me thousands! Yet Melissa acted as if Sue was a monster and demanded

Sue apologise. Sue stood there with her mouth opening and shutting, gulping like one of Matt's guppies! I intervened. Melissa became a fragile, weeping creature, moaning that I didn't love her if I could allow her children to be insulted. . .'

Amy dared to look at West.

'Harem mentality! I finally came to my senses, told her that despite the flaw in her logic she was right, I didn't love her, and insisted she apologise to Sue. She did so, then wept that she wanted to go home to her husband. When she made the call, she told him her mother was much better, and that they would return as soon as possible. He believed she was in Brisbane! My secretary checked timetables and connections and took them to the airport. I've been sitting in my office for half an hour trying to find the courage to face you. I've been a fool.' The closing act of *The Magic Flute* crescendoed in the sudden silence. 'Like Papageno!'

'West?' She was shivering and he put his arms around her.

'Amy. I'm trying to tell you that I love you. I'm sorry, I've taken so long to realise how precious you are to me.' He lowered his head and she closed her eyes and felt the gentle pressure of his lips on her eyelids, the magic of his mouth touch her own, and as she responded his hands drew her body closer. Her own fingers played with the contours of his face and jawline, curling around his ears, then swept possessively from the breadth of his shoulders down to the neat curve of his buttocks.

'Seducing me, my little Amy? You will make an honest man of me and marry me,' he murmured as he nuzzled her ear.

Amy knew her answer. Any man who could call her 'little' had to be blinded by love! She felt him unplait her hair. Between lowered lashes she looked at him and saw the tenderness on his face as he freed her hair from the scarf.

'Sweetheart, I'm going to make love to you and bring you red roses until you say yes!'

'There's not even the last rose of summer in the garden!' Amy murmured, kissing the distracting, windburnt V of skin at the base of his throat, conscious of his growing desire and the pulse of his heart. 'I want you to keep making love to me so I'll have to avoid saying yes!' She loved the rich, deep sound as his chuckle resonated in his chest and the possessive intimacy of his lips on hers. The sound of the closing bars of the opera made them look at each other and smile. Amy felt his warmth as he gently moved to hold her in the crook of his arm.

'Jack O'Day, Come, carry, boy,' he called.

Looking at the door, Amy realised West had left it open a crack and, as she watched, Jack O'Day walked in, carrying a basket on which lay a perfect red rose.

'The *Symbol of Love*, the international name to register for our rose, my sweetheart. Agree?'

'Yes! Yes, of course!'

'You said yes!' His dark eyes teased her with love but he bent, patted Jack and picked up the rose.

'So I did!' she smiled.

West presented the rose. As their hands joined to hold the flower, neither noticed Jack O'Day settle contentedly by the stove. He knew he was home!

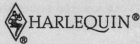
HARLEQUIN®

Don't miss these Harlequin favorites by some of our most distinguished authors!
And now you can receive a discount by ordering two or more titles!

HT#25593	WHAT MIGHT HAVE BEEN by Glenda Sanders	$2.99 U.S. ☐ /$3.50 CAN. ☐
HP#11713	AN UNSUITABLE WIFE by Lindsay Armstrong	$2.99 U.S. ☐ /$3.50 CAN. ☐
HR#03356	BACHELOR'S FAMILY by Jessica Steele	$2.99 U.S.☐ /$3.50 CAN. ☐
HS#70494	THE BIG SECRET by Janice Kaiser	$3.39 ☐
HI#22196	CHILD'S PLAY by Bethany Campbell	$2.89 ☐
HAR#16553	THE MARRYING TYPE by Judith Arnold	$3.50 U.S. ☐ /$3.99 CAN. ☐
HH#28844	THE TEMPTING OF JULIA by Maura Seger	$3.99 U.S ☐ /$4.50 CAN. ☐

(limited quantities available on certain titles)

AMOUNT	$
DEDUCT: 10% DISCOUNT FOR 2+ BOOKS	$
POSTAGE & HANDLING	$
($1.00 for one book, 50¢ for each additional)	
APPLICABLE TAXES*	$
TOTAL PAYABLE	$
(check or money order—please do not send cash)	

To order, complete this form and send it, along with a check or money order for the total above, payable to Harlequin Books, to: **In the U.S.:** 3010 Walden Avenue, P.O. Box 9047, Buffalo, NY 14269-9047; **In Canada:** P.O. Box 613, Fort Erie, Ontario, L2A 5X3.

Name: _____

Address: _____ City: _____

State/Prov.: _____ Zip/Postal Code: _____

*New York residents remit applicable sales taxes.
Canadian residents remit applicable GST and provincial taxes.

HBACK-OD2

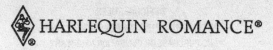

HARLEQUIN ROMANCE®

brings you

Romances that take the family to heart!

Coming next month from Jessica Steele is
THE SISTER SECRET (#3385), our Family Ties book
for November. The "tie" here is rather special—Belvia
and Josy are twin sisters!

But though they look alike, they're chalk and cheese when
it comes to their characters. Josy has always been painfully
shy, while Belvia…well, she isn't afraid of speaking her
mind.

When sisters are in a tight spot they stick together. Josy
has a secret that Belvia is determined to keep. And that
means keeping Josy away from Latham Tavenner.
Unfortunately, the family firm needs Latham's help. Belvia
has no alternative than to attract Latham's attention.
Latham knows exactly which sister he wants. But he's not
about to let Belvia know that!

**Look out for Josy's story in A WIFE IN WAITING,
coming soon from Harlequin Romance.**

OFFICIAL RULES

PRIZE SURPRISE SWEEPSTAKES 3448

NO PURCHASE OR OBLIGATION NECESSARY

Three Harlequin Reader Service 1995 shipments will contain respectively, coupons for entry into three different prize drawings, one for a Panasonic 31" wide-screen TV, another for a 5-piece Wedgwood china service for eight and the third for a Sharp ViewCam camcorder. To enter any drawing using an Entry Coupon, simply complete and mail according to directions.

There is no obligation to continue using the Reader Service to enter and be eligible for any prize drawing. You may also enter any drawing by hand printing the words "Prize Surprise," your name and address on a 3"x5" card and the name of the prize you wish that entry to be considered for (i.e., Panasonic wide-screen TV, Wedgwood china or Sharp ViewCam). Send your 3"x5" entries via first-class mail (limit: one per envelope) to: Prize Surprise Sweepstakes 3448, c/o the prize you wish that entry to be considered for, P.O. Box 1315, Buffalo, NY 14269-1315, USA or P.O. Box 610, Fort Erie, Ontario L2A 5X3, Canada.

To be eligible for the Panasonic wide-screen TV, entries must be received by 6/30/95; for the Wedgwood china, 8/30/95; and for the Sharp ViewCam, 10/30/95.

Winners will be determined in random drawings conducted under the supervision of D.L. Blair, Inc., an independent judging organization whose decisions are final, from among all eligible entries received for that drawing. Approximate prize values are as follows: Panasonic wide-screen TV ($1,800); Wedgwood china ($840) and Sharp ViewCam ($2,000). Sweepstakes open to residents of the U.S. (except Puerto Rico) and Canada, 18 years of age or older. Employees and immediate family members of Harlequin Enterprises, Ltd., D.L. Blair, Inc., their affiliates, subsidiaries and all other agencies, entities and persons connected with the use, marketing or conduct of this sweepstakes are not eligible. Odds of winning a prize are dependent upon the number of eligible entries received for that drawing. Prize drawing and winner notification for each drawing will occur no later than 15 days after deadline for entry eligibility for that drawing. Limit: one prize to an individual, family or organization. All applicable laws and regulations apply. Sweepstakes offer void wherever prohibited by law. Any litigation within the province of Quebec respecting the conduct and awarding of the prizes in this sweepstakes must be submitted to the Regies des loteries et Courses du Quebec. In order to win a prize, residents of Canada will be required to correctly answer a time-limited arithmetical skill-testing question. Value of prizes are in U.S. currency.

Winners will be obligated to sign and return an Affidavit of Eligibility within 30 days of notification. In the event of noncompliance within this time period, prize may not be awarded. If any prize or prize notification is returned as undeliverable, that prize will not be awarded. By acceptance of a prize, winner consents to use of his/her name, photograph or other likeness for purposes of advertising, trade and promotion on behalf of Harlequin Enterprises, Ltd., without further compensation, unless prohibited by law.

For the names of prizewinners (available after 12/31/95), send a self-addressed, stamped envelope to: Prize Surprise Sweepstakes 3448 Winners, P.O. Box 4200, Blair, NE 68009.

RPZ KAL